nahoonkara

a novel

Etruscan Press
Wilkes University
84 West South Street
Wilkes-Barre, PA 18766

 WILKES UNIVERSITY

www.etruscanpress.org

Printed in the United States of America

Library of Congress Cataloging-in-Publication Data

Grandbois, Peter.

Nahoonkara : a novel / by Peter Grandbois. ~ 1st ed.

p. cm.

ISBN 978-0-9819687-6-6 (alk. paper)

1. Magic realism (Literature) I. Title.

PS3607.R3626N34 2011

813'.6-dc22

2010042720

First Edition

Cover photo by Gary Isaacs
Design by Michael Ress

Etruscan Press is committed to sustainability and environmental stewardship. We
elected to print this title through Bookmobile on FSC paper that contains 30%
post consumer fiber manufactured using biogas energy and 100% wind power.

nahoonkara

a novel

Peter Grandbois

etruscan press

For Mom & Dad

nahoonkara

The Players

The Gerrull Family

Margaret "Meg" Gerrull *married to Ernest Gerrull*

Children:
1. Killian
2. Eli *married to Charlotte,*
   Children: Alice and Jane
3. Henry *married to Elizabeth "Nell"*
   Children: Henry Jr., Webb, and Molly
4. Catherine

Uncle Frank *(Margaret's brother)*
Uncle Robert *(Margaret's brother)*

Characters in Whitelake, Wisconsin *(in order of appearance)*

Jake Mulenbach *(suitor to Margaret)*
One-Eared Louie *(a farmer)*
Doctor Apfelbeck
Judge Salt
Oscar Kepsky *(furrier)*
Miss Olivia Hull *(the schoolteacher)*
Bert Allar *(farmer)*
Mr. & Mrs. Lukowicz *(farmers)*
Father Blanchard

Characters in Denver, Colorado *(in order of appearance)*

Elizabeth "Nell" *(adopted daughter of Bertram; Henry's wife)*
Bertram Wheeler *married to Blanche*
(bank owner and adoptive father of Elizabeth)

Characters in Seven Falls, Colorado *(in order of appearance)*

Peter Myers *(first sheriff of Seven Falls, later owner of the general store)*
Carl Cluskey *(owner of the dance hall) married to Ellen*
Children: Ruby (oldest of three)
J.D. Demings *(owner of the hotel) married to Mary*
Martin Watson *(smithy)*
Tom Guller *(saloon owner)*
Percy Hart *(saloon owner)*
Lulu Giberson *married to Galway*
Frank Foote *(fiddle player)*
Jess Carter *(midwife, lives in Montezuma)*
Wellington Taylor *(the mesmerist)*
Antoinette *(the mesmerist's assistant)*
Wallace *(sheriff of Seven Falls)*
Charlotte *(a prostitute/dance hall girl; Eli's wife)*
Dee *(Ute girl saved by Wallace and given a new name by Elizabeth)*
Isaac Hamlin *(an architect from San Francisco)*

The Miners of the "Mad Meg"

Will Markey *(foreman of the mine)*
Jim Leek *(known as Big Jim)*
Silas Cordley
Fitch Wise *(an Englishman, beheaded in his tent)*
Wilbert Marshall *(a drunk preacher)*
Tom Thomas *(known as Double Tom)*
Ben York *(attacks the Ute family along with an unnamed drifter)*

We are like the spider. We weave our life and then move along in it.
We are like the dreamer who dreams and then lives in the dream.

—Aitareya Upanishad

Life is a succession of habits, since the individual is
a succession of individuals.

—Samuel Beckett

Also by Peter Grandbois

The Gravedigger

The Arsenic Lobster: A Hybrid Memoir

nahoonkara

a novel

PROLOGUE
KILLIAN | *Colorado*

I don't know how many souls I have. Each day I wake and find another in the things that shine. And the marsh-grass behind my house shines, the wind that shakes the tavern roof at night shines, the leaves of the cottonwoods by the river shine with green fire. The shining confuses me until memories fall to dreams. But it doesn't end there. The dreams mix with the moon and the clouds, the smell of wild ginger along the riverbank, the taste of dark loam beneath the porch. It's the same whether I dream during the day or at night. And it doesn't matter if my eyes are open or closed. Either way, it's as if I don't exist. Only memories of dreams remain. Like the beehive deep in the hollow log beyond the birch grove. The buzzing makes me feel less lonely. So I crawl up close to the blinding fire. The bees come and go, their legs taking the sun from their backs and shaping it, making more cells, more body. Or like the black river, colors mixed like licorice in sassafras, her body outlined upon the bottom, stones spilling from her pockets. The damp air the only smell left. A five-lined skink runs along the bank. I follow it. He stops on the mossy rock at the water's edge, waits patiently for his evening meal. White foam rises upon the black, licking a branch from the shore. I watch it float, hoping to learn. But I can find no lesson worth remembering.

And then, sometimes, the memories blend. One by one the bees sting me. I watch them writhing in the dirt. The skink's tongue strikes the air, even as dusk falls, a harsh blow upon my skin. I peek inside the log once more just to be certain I'm dreaming. The skink is gone. I stand in its place upon the rock, searching the river's roiling depths, arm stretching toward the icy water. It's then I know that the bees lying silently on the ground will reemerge from the cells of the hive, like Uncle Frank from the whale. And they do.

ONE

THE TAVERN
Wisconsin

Drift down through the snowy rooftop to the Wisconsin tavern of 1854 where his memories begin. Do you recognize the harsh tang of sweat, hops, and wood smoke? Do you hear the strum of the guitar and the breathy oom-pah-pah of the accordion? Do you see the smoke as it climbs the air, swirling about the nearly perfect web stretched between the roof beams? Do you feel the web vibrate, pulsing in time with the music, see the orb weaver in the center? She is there, waiting.

Float through the buzz of people. Look at Meg, his mother. She turns bright red as she laughs. By ten, she'll be red as a turnip and ready to pass out. Then she'll sit and fan herself, swaying back and forth on the pine bench, her body a bellows moving the much needed air. And there's his father, standing on the chair in the far corner, strumming his guitar, dark hair falling over gray eyes, sweat pouring from his face, big patches discoloring his armpits. Do you see the pain limning his mouth? Get a good look. He doesn't show it often. And Uncle Frank standing beside him, his arm around his brother's shoulders as he belts out another tune. Uncle Robert sits in another chair, working the accordion as if he's conjuring spirits.

How to find the beginning? Don't bother. It would be better to sift through the smoke, follow the wisps, searching for a strand of story. Maybe you'll find a strand that is rich. But then again, maybe not. Maybe it goes nowhere. Maybe the story you pull from the air is only important to the teller. Or maybe you believe that a piece of the whole lies in even the most insignificant shred. Take for example the story of Jake Mulenbach. He loved Killian's mother. Still does, though he tries to hide it when he sits beside her children. Look. Now, as he brings the sodas to the children, as if he could still win

them over, could still be their father. He walks with a limp. We
don't know why. He stops, sets the tray down and combs his hair
over in a vain attempt to cover his bald spot. He is dressed in his
Sunday best, though it's Thursday. Look, but don't be too obvious.
He's skittrel, like a squirrel. And we want him to tell his story. Need
him to. There. He sits on the bench beneath the farming tools,
the tacks and harnesses, rakes and forks, the mill grinder and corn
sheller. Look how he gathers the children about him. Seven-year-
old Eli is there first, climbing into Jake's lap, his blonde hair falling
over his dark eyes. Eli loves stories. Needs them as we do, you'll see.
Five-year-old Henry approaches more cautiously. He doesn't like
Jake's story because it doesn't make sense. Henry asks too many
questions, wanting to understand. He probably wouldn't listen at
all if it weren't for the sodas. Do you see Killian, the oldest of the
brothers, standing to the side, watching everything, one hand in
his overall pocket, the other holding the hand of his baby sister,
Catherine. He loves stories too, but he can't help standing apart.
He'll take little Catherine closer, but he won't sit. It's how he is.

Watch as Jake pulls out his corncob pipe, as he fills it and tamps
it down. Listen as he talks of the labors of the past week, his worries
for the coming summer, how he's got to find a better way to irrigate.
Be patient. It's important to wait and watch. And most of all to
listen to the roiling voices. You didn't think there'd be just one, did
you? Even if it looks and sounds like one voice, it's just an illusion,
a storyteller's trick.

"Tell us about the horses," Eli says. Like so many children, he
asks for the same story over and over, even though the fact that
Jake never finishes it drives him crazy. It doesn't matter. Killian will
finish it for him, later. He'll make up his own ending, and who is
to say it didn't actually happen that way?

"You want that old story again?" Jake asks as he passes his pipe in
front of his nose, inhaling deeply.

The children nod. Killian watches. Catherine breaks from him
and steps forward, eyes wide.

"It all started," Jake says, "the day your Uncle Robert gave me permission to visit his sister." He puts the pipe in his mouth and puffs, considering. "And the very next day your father was over at her house, sitting high atop his horse and talking with her through the window. I saw the whole thing and couldn't believe it."

"Was that horse one of the crazy ones?" Henry asks, though he knows the answer. He tucks himself in closer to Jake.

"Your Uncle Robert had just got himself a young team after making a deal to buy this tavern," Jake goes on. "He was so proud he took Meg, I mean your mother, for a ride down Main Street on a Sunday afternoon." He puffs again before continuing. The rich, fudge scent mixes with wood smoke in the rafters. "They'd made a right on Second and run smack dab into your father's pelt cart parked in front of Kepsky's Furrier."

"This is the part I don't like," Henry says, covering his ears.

Jake places a hand on Henry's head, strokes his hair. "They say the moment your father came out of Kepsky's the horses took fright."

"Why'd they do that?" Henry asks.

We told you he would ask too many questions. Eli sits lost in the dream. Killian is already finishing the story in his head, imagining what he'll tell the others.

"I don't know," Jake replies. "All I know is that them horses swung around in front of Kepsky's and tore off back the way they came, running right over Judge Salt's lawn."

Meg returns from the kitchen, carrying a plate of raspberry pie to her husband as he sits playing the guitar. Jake follows her with his eyes. Turns his pipe around and around in his hands as if considering the shape of it.

"Go on," Eli says.

Jake looks wide-eyed like he's lost the thread of story, but then quickly takes it up again. "The buggy's wheel hit the base of the Judge's big elm and the buggy tipped, spilling your mother and

Uncle Robert onto the lawn. Your mother hit her head on an exposed root and was knocked unconscious."

"Was she okay?" Henry asks.

"She was fine," Jake replies. "But I'll get to her in a second. You see the horses didn't stop there; they continued on down Spence Street, dragging the remains of the buggy behind them until they collided with John July's barn. The lead horse fell down dazed, then got back up and ran into the barn again."

"What scared them so?" Henry asks.

Jake stares into the cooling ashes of his pipe. "Your father was the first to arrive, he says finally. "He helped your uncle get your mother inside the Judge's house. I was supposed to have come over for dinner that evening," he says. "But of course, everything was cancelled." He puffs hard in an attempt to rekindle the ashes.

Henry takes a sip from his Birch Bark Soda. Catherine tries to steal it away until Killian steps forward and points out she has her own.

"What happened to the horses?" Eli asks. His own soda has gone untouched.

Jake knocks the cold ashes from his pipe onto the floor and sits staring into the smoky haze. "It don't matter," he says. "Not anymore it don't. One thing can go and change everything until you don't know who you are or what you could have been, until nothing seems to matter at all." ·

"Why don't you just tell the story different next time?" Killian asks, but no one pays attention.

Meg sits beside her husband as the musicians take a break. Eli kicks at the sawdust on the floor, frustrated he can never find out about the horses. Jake rises and goes over to talk with Uncle Frank by the kitchen door. Henry knocks over Eli's soda in an attempt to steal Jake's spot. Catherine sips her Sarsaparilla with brown-stained lips. She takes Killian's hand once again, and Killian squeezes it to acknowledge her presence. He must do this because he is inhaling the fading fudge scent of Jake's pipe. It drifts in the air about him, and he follows it upward. But when he peers through the rafters all he sees are the broken tendrils of web swaying back and forth as if pushed by an unseen hand.

SEVEN FALLS
Narrator | *Colorado*

Here now is the recorded history of Seven Falls, how it came to be. The children are grown, though this story moves back and forth as you have probably already guessed. Watch how Henry passes through the Great Plains with Killian in tow. Look how he moves without surcease, hematite summoned by the magnetic call of the Rocky Mountains. The prairie means nothing to him. The rangy beasts. The dirty birds rising from the darkening plain. The ragged encampments of Indians or settlers. Only the red rock that lines the eastern wall of the Rockies sears itself into his dreams, night after night, as he crosses the plains.

Let us traverse the spine of the world with them and dip down into a valley that stretches north to south. Its western edge running up against three mountains huddled together like witches over a cauldron.

Two rivers flow between the mountains, joining at their base. Listen, as Killian names the river made from this confluence the Blue because of the pure color of its water. Hear, as he names the first and strongest of its tributaries Seven Falls for its steep passage and seven drops. The second Snake for its winding path.

Do you see how Henry talks with the handful of Mexicans who make the valley their home, the way he finds common ground in the language of rock and earth? We drift up the three mountains together with them. We share their methods for testing the sheared rock. We follow trails of granite to denser minerals within, opening veins of galena, acanthite, and quartz, always looking for the telltale signs of silver.

The Mexicans tell us that the three mountains are known together as "Tres Hermanas Arpías," but that each also has its own name and the southernmost is called La Nana. What they don't tell us is that the mountain's full name is La Nana Bruja. But we know better. Henry lays his claim about a third of the way up the face of the Old Witch and names the mine Meg after his mother.

Word of the mine's potential spreads fast—as word of money always does—and caravan after caravan arrives filled with miners and store and saloon keeps ready to service them. Bankers, lawyers, blacksmiths, and even a few dancehall girls follow.

Of course, fights break out. It is inevitable. At first they are rare, but soon nearly every day. Henry doesn't like this. Killian is already apart from it all, lost in the woods above the town, watching from afar as one miner stabs a Mexican through the eye with a broken bottle. Do you see the Mexican there, twitching in the street? How no one clears his body from the mud until the following morning and then only because a cartload of hammers can't get through? It is then Henry decides to call a meeting.

Listen with Killian from the corner of the room.

"We are a community now," Henry tells the crowd stuffed into Guller's Saloon. "And we need to start acting like one. The first thing we need is a name."

"What we need are women," Pete Myers shouts from somewhere in the crowd.

"What you need's a horse," someone else shouts.

"Now, I propose we do this democratically," Henry says once the laughter dies down. "Let each man write down the name he thinks best."

"But Tom can't write," a man shouts.

"Neither can Frank," another says.

"Seven Falls." A man with a goose-bone pipe in his mouth stands up in the center of the room and repeats the name. "Seven Falls." The man's leathered skin so crosshatched with lines it looks like a fighting cock has been let loose upon it.

"Your brother named the river that feeds this town, and it's as good a name as any," the man says, his pipe clenched firmly in his mouth as he speaks.

Henry says nothing, transfixed by the web of smoke emanating from the man's pipe, the way it drifts about us. It's the same rich, fudge scent as Jake Mulenbach's tobacco.

"The name's Will," the man says. "Will Markey." Watch as they vote Will Markey sheriff. Listen as he turns it down, saying he was born to work the mines. Meet Pete Myers, who foolishly steps up for the job.

"The next thing we need is a school teacher," Henry says. "We can't have a proper town without a school."

"But we ain't got but three kids, and they're all Carl's property," Pete Myers offers.

Henry stands upon a chair as if he could better see through the smoky haze. He notes the lack of Mexicans. The fact that they've already cleared out. "That's going to change," he says. "That's all going to change."

Let us listen now to other voices as we ride the smoke round and round, round and round, until we are diminished.

WHY WE FORGET
KILLIAN | *Wisconsin*

"Look!" Catherine shouts when she spies the river. It's springtime, and the river rushes with the force of the snowmelt. "Water!" she screams. Catherine points the way to the wide banks of the Big Eau Pleine. Even though she's three, it's she who leads me, her wobbly gait my guide.

Eli wouldn't take the time to follow a three-year-old through the woods, to give himself up to a child who meanders like the river, moving from flower to flower, from insect to insect and rock to rock, saying she's a butterfly and not really human at all. Henry might do it for a time, but not trusting in her, he'd want to go his own way.

She steps to the edge of the river, wanting to get as close as she can. Leaning into the cold mist, she teeters on the brink, and I pull her back. I don't want to because I know she's alive just then with the mist in her face. I can feel it. But I do it anyway. Someone has to fear. I suppose that once we're at the river our roles reverse to the way they should be, and I'm her guardian and guide.

I point to the calm, shady pools near the bank where the fish feel protected. I tell her that no matter how wild the river the fish can always find a safe place to hide. What I don't tell her is that it's the first thing a young fisherman learns, and so it's the first place he'll look.

I don't know if I can explain it, but I feel as if Catherine is my own child, not my sister, that once we walk past the line of elms that marks our property, things change.

We go to the river every day after my chores are done, every day for a year. When you see a river that much, it's easy to see its patterns—the rush and swell of spring as the river charges over boulders, carrying away branches, not concerned with working its way around things because it has the strength to run right over them. And then summer. Catherine told me once she could see the sun stealing the river's breath in the summer. In fall, we count the leaves floating down, watching them get stuck on a rock where the river's low. I tell her that the river senses the long sleep of winter—my favorite time of year—and prepares for it. She loves winter too, but not for the same reason I do. She loves the way the falling snow feels on her face. I tell her how most people think of winter as death, that people think underneath all that snow and ice the river dies. But the river's waiting, that's all.

I remember a day just after Christmas, with two feet of snow already covering everything. Catherine can't walk through the snow, so I carry her on my shoulders. She says she likes being a giant, looking down at the earth from the treetops. But then she spots a deer half buried in the snow, not moving. I figure it hasn't been there long because the coyotes haven't gotten to it yet. I want to take a closer look, but I don't. This is another thing I don't want Catherine to see. Though maybe it's better if she does.

She asks right away why the deer doesn't move, and I don't have an answer. I tell her the deer is sleeping, just like Mother tells me when I ask her to explain death.

Ice-fingers stretch across the surface. Still, the water rushes through, always finding a way. We sit on the bank in the snow, and I wonder at the clarity of it. The cold somehow seems essential. You'd think it would be the other way around, that a frozen world would cloud until all definition is lost.

A brown speckled trout treads the still shallow by the bank. "Is he sleeping like the deer?" Catherine asks. I stare at the trout and have to wonder myself; he's so still.

"No," I say. "His sleep is different." To make her forget, I distract her like I've seen Mother do, point out a spot where the water flows over the ice rather than under.

"How?" Catherine asks. And I wonder at how she knows, how children always seem to know when you're lying or distracting them from the things that matter. I can't answer her, so I stare at the trout. Then Catherine asks what happens to the trout when the snow comes and the river freezes over.

"It waits, sleeping under the ice," I say.

"Is the deer waiting, too?"

I don't have an answer for her. And I know what Mother feels like those days when I ask her all sorts of questions. As soon as you start looking, you see that most things don't have answers, only questions and more questions. Children understand that. That's why they never linger too long on any one question; there are too many others to ask.

Every time we come to the river it's different. There are the big changes that follow the seasons, but there are also smaller changes, ones you can only catch if you visit every day the way Catherine and I do—the slight rise and fall of the level marked by the bank; the choices the river makes on which way to go around a rock, (or simply to go over it); the sounds shifting from a ripple to a babble to a gush depending on the river's mood. I find myself wondering if it's the river that changes every day, or if we do. That's what I want to ask Catherine. But I think she's too young. I don't know then that we're born understanding and only with time do we forget. By the time we die, everything is a mystery.

THE PROCESS OF SEDIMENTATION
Henry | Colorado

I was walking into Wheeler's Bank, looking to get a loan for more supplies, when she came through the door, head lowered so that all I could see was her wide-brimmed hat with a red ribbon around the top. I would have kept going had the earth not spoken. I would have passed by, never knowing that the wide-brimmed hat was all that held the fragments and that the woman beneath that hat had just about given up hope of someone coming along to gather the parts of her and hold them together. But the earth shifted beneath my feet, and I pay attention to any geologic alteration. I stopped, pulled the handkerchief from my pocket, and gathered her inside.

"I'm looking for a schoolteacher," I said. "One who doesn't mind the hardships of the mountains."

"A bank is a funny place to find one." She kept her head down, her hat tilted to the side like a shield.

"Can you help me?"

"It depends," she replied. "Are those your initials on your handkerchief?"

"Pardon my manners," I said, offering my hand. "My name's Henry Gerrull."

"I'm Elizabeth," she said, her hand rising to meet mine. "Elizabeth . . . " She repeated, then hesitated, as if searching the layers of her own history.

"Just Elizabeth?" I spread the handkerchief over her hand.

"Yes."

I placed my hand upon the handkerchief, took her hand in mine. "Well, Elizabeth is a grand enough name to carry the weight of two," I said. "And I'm guessing that your face is beautiful enough to warrant such a name." Her head remained bowed, but the handkerchief trembled between us.

"A pleasure to meet you," she said, stepping away from me and out the door.

The handkerchief floated to the ground.

I didn't bother to pick it up, hoping to catch a glimpse of her as she reached the end of the boardwalk. She hiked up her skirts just enough to avoid the ever-present mud and crossed with a determination I would not have expected from one with so fine a hat. On the surface, she appeared a lady. But underneath, there were places chiseled hard and sharp. She had seen much of the world. Enough, at least, not to bother waiting for a man to throw his coat down over the mud.

Denver was not so big at the time that a few well-placed questions couldn't locate a person. Divining rare minerals beneath the earth was far more difficult than finding a lady in the newly formed city. I soon learned that the family of Bertram Wheeler, the banker, had adopted Elizabeth years ago. No one I talked to knew her last name, who her family had been, nor even how long she'd been living with the Wheelers.

Though the "Meg" had not yet struck a definitive vein, the next day I filled my bags with what ore I had, marched into Wheeler's office, and dropped the bags upon his desk with a thud.

"People won't remember gold once the 'Meg' hits what I know she's going to hit," I told Wheeler as I pulled a piece of snake-like silver from the bag.

"A highly unlikely scenario," Wheeler said, delicately taking the silver from my hand with his thick fingers and sniffing it. "Talk in town, Mr. Gerrull, is that you don't know what you're doing up there." He tasted the silver then, flakes of it falling in his dark beard.

"And what do you think?" I laid my last bag of silver on his desk to weigh his position in my favor.

"I think you've got balls of silver, Mr. Gerrull," Wheeler said, laughing. He extended his hand, and I took it, wishing I had not left my handkerchief upon the floor of his bank, as his palm was covered in sweat.

"You're a shrewd man, Mr. Wheeler."

"Just don't prove me wrong," he replied, pocketing the silver. "A present for my daughter."

"I didn't know you were a family man," I said, seeing my opening. "I'm sure your daughter is quite a charmer."

"That and more, Mr. Gerrull," he replied, reaching out and pulling another piece of the delicate silver from my bag, then wrapping his thick fingers about it.

"Can I buy you a drink?" I offered.

"I've got a better idea," he replied, taking the bait. "Why don't you come for dinner at my house?"

"Wonderful!" I said, thinking that I had just struck two veins with one blow of my hammer.

Elizabeth did not appear until just before dinner. Bertram (he insisted I call him that) and I passed the time in the smoking room while the servants prepared the meal and the women prepared themselves. Mrs. Blanche Wheeler greeted us first, a beautiful woman in the way that ice holds beauty, in the fineness of its features, the pale clarity of its surface. The starched collar of her dress pushed her head high, perfectly aligned with the straight set of her spine. She offered me her hand, and, as I kissed it, I looked for imperfections, cracks in her veneer, but the skin clung so tightly to the bone that what thin lines she had did not go deep.

Blanche called Elizabeth down twice before she made her appearance. Though I had been allowed plenty of time to gather myself, I was not prepared for the odd sadness that pierces through eyes of dark green light. And though I'd seen her hands before, I could not have been ready for the way in which a man can lose himself in the forest of brown hair that falls black upon a milky shoulder.

"Pleased to meet you, Mr. Gerrull," she said, once again giving me her hand.

Without the protection of my handkerchief, I was left exposed. I extended my hand, attempting to clasp hers only to stop short, leaving but a little air between our fingers to be shaped, like a piece of clay, from the possibility of our desire. Elizabeth's face betrayed nothing, as if it was still hidden by her wide-brimmed hat. But I sensed the gazes of Bertram and his wife as they observed the effect their adopted daughter had on their guest. It was then Bertram stepped between us, displacing the air before I could discern its shape. I remember that I couldn't tell whether his action was a gesture of fatherly protection or the jealous stance of a threatened lover.

"Henry is a miner," Bertram practically shouted from his position at the end of the long mahogany dining table.

"A geologist," I corrected him. "Trained at Harvard. I'm here to test my theories, and so far they are proving correct."

"As long as they prove profitable," Bertram replied, taking a long sip of wine.

"I thought geology was a discredited science," Mrs. Wheeler interjected. "We all know that the earth was created in seven days, that humans have only been around a few thousand years. How silly it all is to suggest that rocks are millions of years old." She laughed, tilting her thin nose to the side so that it appeared the beak of a bird.

"Pardon me for saying so, Mrs. Wheeler, but if humans continue with such thoughts we'll never step out of the Dark Ages. The evidence in favor of an Earth that predates man is simply overwhelming. And for that we owe a debt of gratitude to geologists like Sir Charles Lyell." I had spoken before thinking better of it, and now it was too late. I hoped to steal a glance at Elizabeth, to get a hint of where she stood, to know that if I had alienated myself from my hosts, I had at least not lost her.

"I've never understood the English," Bertram interrupted. "To all appearances they seem a God-fearing race, but then they produce devils like Darwin and Lyell."

It was as if I were sitting in the woods during the cold light of early morning, watching my father stand with his back to me, rifle raised, searching the sky. Where was the language that was my own, the one I had fought so hard to find? How could I speak and not lose all?

"What do you think, Elizabeth?" I asked, surprising myself. There was silence as all eyes focused on her. She kept her hands in her lap, her head lowered. It was then I regretted my haste.

"I don't see why we can't believe in both," she said, and all at that table leaned forward to hear. "We can certainly accept the teachings of science without shattering our faith."

No one moved. I sensed by the coolness in Blanche's gaze and the tight set of Bertram's mouth that this was the first time Elizabeth had contradicted, even if ever so slightly, her adopted parents.

Preferring to lose the afterlife rather than a profitable deal, Bertram followed Elizabeth into the middle ground. "There's no need to be obstinate, Blanche," he said. "We are civilized people." Taking up his knife, he cut into his steak and began eating in earnest. The bloody juice pooled on his plate. "Certainly, we can disagree and still enjoy our dinner."

Blanche gazed at her husband with sleeted eyes before finally picking up her fork. "You are right, of course," she said. Her food remained untouched.

When it was over, I thanked them all for a pleasant evening and bid them good night. I waited, hoping for a sign, but Elizabeth stood silently behind her parents. Finally, Mr. and Mrs. Wheeler walked me to the door, where Bertram handed me first my coat, then my hat.

I prepared to leave, Bertram holding the door for me, when her footsteps echoed through the long hall. The air thickened between us, taking shape once again.

"Mr. Gerrull!" she called. "I thought you might need this, as I noticed you were without one of your own."

She stood breathless before me, holding out one of her own blue silk handkerchiefs.

Mr. and Mrs. Wheeler stared on, more surprised than I.

"That is very kind of you," I said, taking the handkerchief from her, this time allowing my hand to linger in the space above hers. The air between us shaped itself into a single phrase, a phrase that went unspoken yet was understood just the same.

The next morning, as I waited in the park along the Platte, I wondered what would have happened had I taken her hand, pressed it in mine. It seemed to me that it would have crumbled, that it was made of sand and would have fallen apart at the slightest pressure. I don't know why I imagined her hand that way. She'd proven herself to be quite strong.

As the morning passed, I waited beneath the biggest cottonwood I could find, but it offered little shade. No time had been mentioned for our meeting, and it was only then I realized that no place had actually been mentioned either. The image of it had simply appeared in my mind.

The sun stared down from its meridian, and I was beginning to think that I would never discover what held her layers together. I wondered if, perhaps, it was best I did not. The overwhelming feeling of the night before came back to me, the thickening of air that nearly suffocated, and I wondered if I was strong enough to withstand the force of her need. I put on my hat, rose, and began crossing through the field of columbines concentrated in the center of the park. There, on the opposite edge of the blue and white flowers, stood Elizabeth, a suitcase in one hand and two hatboxes in the other.

The next coach west wasn't leaving until the following morning, and Bertram would have his men out looking for her once he calmed down. "I want a new name," she'd told him. "And I'm leaving to go look for it." He'd been puffing on his midday cigar, she said, and when he saw my hatboxes he put his cigar out.

We found a hotel on the edge of town and stayed there. I booked two rooms, but after I dropped her off at her door, she followed me to mine. I didn't say anything, and neither did she. This time I did not hesitate. I took her hand in mine, careful to hold it as one might hold a bird.

As sediments pile up, their pressure squeezes the water out and packs the particles together. Sometimes, the minerals laid down between grains cement to create one magnificent mass of rock. I'd studied every kind of rock at Harvard, but I didn't know anything could be as beautiful as the fusing of one's layers with another, the shifting and packing, the reorientation of grains. All through the night, I held her close, hoping the pressure would solidify her, that the friction would smooth the rough edges, reshape the pieces that had not been abraded, but I was new to the ways of love, and I did not know that just because one soul wills something that intention cannot always cross the vast gulf to another. Even if it could, sometimes a body is not porous enough to let it in, sometimes the result of the process of sedimentation is to squeeze everything out.

ANGELS
ELI | *Wisconsin*

I look out through the frost on the living room window each morning before school. I spend hours staring through the fog of crystals until Uncle Frank and Uncle Robert look like shapeless beasts as they shovel the snow out front and Killian becomes a dark shade as he plays with Henry and Catherine beneath the line of elms. I trace patterns in the frost, but I never look through the cleared glass. That would ruin the illusion. Mother says I draw the most beautiful manger she's ever seen. She says she wishes she could take it right off the window and place it under our Christmas tree.

What she doesn't know is that after I trace the baby Jesus lying there amongst all the animals, his mother Mary and Joseph looking on, I trace the devil in the background. I make the devil and Jesus fight for the souls of the animals. Jesus almost always wins.

I trace my manger in the darkness of early morning and wait for the rising sun, the ticking of the grandfather clock behind me creeping across my scalp, breathing its way into my head until the battle begins.

Late at night, when everyone is asleep, I walk through the house, laying my hand upon each clock. Mother loves clocks, and Father sometimes brings her one when he returns from his trips. The others are smaller: there's a Willard Banjo clock on the mantle, a shelf clock on top of the pantry in the kitchen, a Hatch Wall clock in the entryway, and, of course, the big grandfather in the living room—Mother says it's a Brokaw and worth a lot of money. She even kissed Father the day he brought it home. When I lay my hands upon them, it's like the tick tock of the clocks is the breathing of the house. Sometimes I feel like I could bring them to life, like Jesus. But sometimes I try to silence them. Then, when I get tired of that, I lie completely still on the living room sofa and wait.

"Eli, what are you doing sitting there?" Mother asks one night when Father's gone, and she can't sleep. She pulls the star quilt out of the trunk and wraps it around me. I let her do it, but as soon as she sits down, I shirk it off.

"I'm listening to the breath of the Holy Spirit," I say.

She says nothing then, but picks up the quilt and puts it on my shoulders again. It slides off because I wish it to.

"Does the holy spirit breathe through the clocks?" she asks, looking out the window as if she is afraid to look at me.

"Yes," I whisper. I want to tell her about the frost on the windows too, tell her I create it with my breath, that the breath of the Holy Spirit works through me, and I can touch it, use it any way I like. But at that moment, there's another sound, the soft crunching of snow outside, and Mother's attention turns from me. She heads toward the door.

I trace my manger scene upon the window, peering through the frosted pane at Mother and the darker figure talking outside. The tick tocking of the clock marking the eternal struggle. She holds him close before she turns to come back in. I am determined to make sure Jesus wins, so I make Jesus strong so he can throw the devil back into the pit, even though he's just a baby.

A moment later, she stands beside me, offering her hand to take me to bed. The devil creeps behind the roof of my manger. I can feel him there. I try to warn the baby Jesus that he's coming. I hope he can hear my thoughts. Then Mother takes my hand and we ascend the stairs.

The next morning when I wake, I slip quietly down through the darkness, taking my accustomed place upon the sofa.

As the first peelings of light break on the horizon, I notice that my manger scene has frosted over, but you can still make out the pattern. The crystals that formed in the night are different from those of the previous day, blurred, as if the two distinct designs are sewn together.

The sun peers forcefully over the horizon, its orange fire crackling through the frost. It's then it happens. The patchwork frost breaks the light into shimmering figures made of yellows, greens, blues, purples, and reds. And in the images that dance upon the wood floor, I see them there, the angels of light. Creatures born from that frosty breath, from my breath. I know those angels will protect me, and they will protect my mother. Nothing that beautiful could ever be bad.

THE SCHOOLMARM
ELIZABETH | *Colorado*

Henry said I'd make an excellent teacher, and who was I to doubt such a man? And so, when September rolled around, I put on my schoolmarm hat, a pink-knotted straw accented by flowers, and marched down Main Street to the schoolhouse. The town of Seven Falls was still in its infancy, and in the short walk between my house at the west end of town and the school at the east, I passed by all that yet existed in the patch of land we'd carved out under the three mountains. Each morning, I would nod to J.D., who watched the sunrise from the entryway of his hotel, then pass on to Carl's cabin and the Dancehall behind it—the silence of which in the early morning always seemed haunted by the revelry of the night before—then the supply house, Martin Watson's smithy, Pete Myer's general store—Pete liked to stack his fruits and vegetables on the boardwalk outside his store, never realizing that the dogs would pee on them as soon as he stepped back inside. Finally, the two saloons, Tom Guller's and Percy Hart's. There had been three saloons until the month before, when Henry made Ike Prestrud sell his so that the town could turn it into a schoolhouse. At first, Ike wasn't too happy, but then he saw the money Henry offered, laid down in pure silver, and he packed his horse and headed for Denver.

It would take the entire year for the smell of whiskey to vanish from the schoolhouse, and in early September the vapors were so strong you nearly got drunk on them. The five kids that started the school year sat on old whiskey barrels. For the first few months, the bar served as my desk, until Henry got me a proper one. Henry thought my misgivings about being a schoolteacher, my despondency on the slow walk back from the schoolhouse, were the results of the fact that the school still looked like a saloon. And so he did his best to change out the trappings of the miner's nightlife as quickly as possible, importing real desks from the east coast. He thought it was an exterior problem, a problem of form, as he sees so much of his world.

Each morning, I asked the students to open McGuffey's Reader, and we would read a passage from the Bible, Shakespeare, Defoe, Tennyson, or Byron. We would cover punctuation and articulation, and parse the grammar. Carl's oldest girl, Ruby, was quite adept at spelling and defining the words, and she helped guide the littler ones. She even corrected me the times I became stuck, confused in my new role. No wonder. I have played so many: minister's daughter, banker's mistress, now devoted wife and schoolmarm. There will be more yet to play.

So, when Carl arranged the first dance in his hall (the town could now boast of four women and so a celebration was considered in order), I wore the pink and gray silk dress and matching hat that Henry had bought me as a wedding present. The whole ensemble was like a breath of fine, French perfume.

Carl's Dancehall had originally been his barn, but early that first year both his cows had died and Carl said it wasn't worth the bother to get new ones if he couldn't rely on them to last through the harsh winter. So, he converted his barn into a dancehall. He said if he charged a quarter to get in, he'd make more money that way than off of cattle. Besides, he figured, people always wanted to dance.

Considering the surroundings, Henry and I made a grand entrance. The town's three other women, Lulu Giberson, Ellen Cluskey, and Mary Demings, were already there, wearing their wedding dresses, as they were the nicest dresses they owned. At first it was strange to see them sitting on the hay bales that lined the sides of the hall and served as benches, but soon we all got used to it. The stranger sight was that some of the men came dressed as women, wearing horsehair wigs and skirts sewn hastily together out of potato sacks. They figured they'd be able to dance more this way, as the men refused to dance with other men, unless they were so dressed.

As soon as we arrived, Frank Foote started up his fiddle and J.D. began strumming his guitar. People didn't take to dancing right away, though. First, the men and women separated, lining up on each side of the barn. The liquor had already been pouring profusely, but as soon as they lined up, each side passed the bottles of whiskey around. I'm not sure who drank more, the men dressed as women, thinking they needed to be inebriated if they were going to get through their role, or the men, thinking they needed every last drop if they were going to have to spend the night looking at their unshaven and grimy partners.

Once the dancing commenced, I couldn't stop laughing. The site of Tom Guller and Martin Watson carrying on—Tom acting the lady—was enough to put everyone in a fine mood. I danced with Pete Myers, Percy Hart, and Big Jim Leek, while Henry smoked a cigar and talked with the men in the corner. I worked up such a sweat that I took off my hat.

"You hold this, Henry," I said. "I won't be needing it anymore this evening."

Henry put out his cigar and stared, perhaps trying to decipher what new role I'd adopted. "You are a vision of elegance tonight, Elizabeth," he said. Then, when I thought he might say more, he took my hat and placed it upon Silas Cordley's head. "You see," Henry went on. "It's not the hat that makes the person, it's the person that gives beauty to the hat, and Silas here has no beauty to spare!"

"Why don't you dance with your wife," Silas replied, still wearing the hat, "unless you want to dance with me?" And with that Silas curtsied and stuck out his hand.

Henry pulled the handkerchief from his breast pocket, laying it on his own hand before taking mine. "Will you do me the honor, my dear?"

I nodded my head in answer, and we walked to the dance floor, careful to avoid the bodies leaping and twirling about us. Once in the center of the room, we stopped and turned to face each other. Henry kept the handkerchief in his hand as he placed his arm around me.

"What are you going to do with your other hand?" I asked, smiling as if I were joking. "Do you have another handkerchief in your pocket for that one?"

Henry smiled uncomfortably. "I'm sorry, dear," he said. "I'm not sure what to do."

"You take my hand in your own," I replied.

"Yes, of course." Carefully, he reached for my hand.

"And then you move to the music."

"But, I don't know how," he replied, attempting to pull me closer.

"Then, I'll show you."

Frank and J.D. started up the next tune, and I kicked up my heels, Henry trying his best to follow along. At first, I didn't mind teaching him how to dance. He was so like a boy set in a room full of grownups and told to mind himself. So we danced, and I gazed smilingly into his eyes. We were husband and wife. What did it matter if we couldn't dance together? The important thing was to try. I let Henry lead, and he pushed and pulled me along, all the while remaining in the center of the room. All around us bodies spinning and jumping. I focused on Henry's eyes, thinking that would give me the illusion of movement. But the more I looked into them, the more we seemed to slow, until I was sure we'd come to a full stop right there in the center of the room. It was then I felt his handkerchief upon my back, absorbing the sweat so that it wouldn't touch his hand, and it was then I realized how light his touch was upon my other hand, as if he were afraid of squeezing me too hard, afraid I might break.

That night, Henry and I made love, though I was never sure why or how it happened. It was not like the first time. Rather, it seemed as if he needed to reach out, to explain himself after the dance, and lying on top of me, pushing into me, seemed like the best kind of explanation.

I have heard that when some people murmur through the dark grammar of their lives, they actually believe they understand. That hope is what led me to the schoolhouse, the hope that by parsing the grammar of others, I could unravel my own life and perhaps follow the signs.

But instead of a lesson from that night, I was left with a child. My first, but not my last. Who knows, maybe this next role will prove to be my greatest. At least I will not have to worry about keeping myself whole, about finding out what's inside. I will have all I can handle to keep my children from unraveling themselves.

THE SONG OF HIS PRESENCE
KILLIAN | *Wisconsin*

In the frail light of deep winter, I hold Catherine close, two bears beneath the blankets. She tells me she has nightmares, and I kick them away with my feet, slap at them with my hands.

Eli and Henry share the other bed. Henry's either stolen the covers or Eli's kicked free of them. I think he kicks away nightmares, too. Only they are his own, and if you sleep in the bed with him, he'll kick you as well. That's why Catherine won't sleep with them. She says Henry sweats and Eli kicks. That's why she sleeps with me.

There are only two rooms atop the tavern, the children in one, the adults in the other, Mother and Father sharing one bed, Uncle Robert and Uncle Frank the other. Mother tells me the only time they didn't share that room was on her wedding night. I ask her why my uncles slept in the hayloft that night, and she laughs. She laughs every time I ask it. I think most nights they're all so tired from working the tavern it doesn't matter where they sleep. But on Sundays the tavern is closed. So, we gather in front of the fireplace in the living room built behind the tavern.

Father is not back from his trip north, so Uncle Robert plays his accordion alone. He gets sweaty, too, sweatier it seems when he plays without Father. And while Uncle Robert plays, Uncle Frank sits thinking about the story he's going to tell, as if he might actually tell a new one. The snow falls heavy, which always makes it seem like the world is being erased.

Mother sits in the chair closest to the fireplace, and I sit at her feet while Catherine sits at mine. I like sitting close to the fire, the way the burning spreads across my back. But mostly I like listening to the crackling of the pine logs. Henry and Eli dance with each other round and round until they exhaust themselves and collapse on the floor.

Just as the pools of sweat under Uncle Robert's arms threaten to spread around to the front and join behind his accordion, Uncle Frank rises from his rocking chair, scratches his head and steps before the fireplace. He searches the ceiling for characters, looks out the window for plots, though it doesn't matter which one, really. I love them all, and he ends them all the same. Whether he starts out in the South Pacific or deep in the woods of the north or adrift in the Aegean Sea, he is soon swallowed up and has to find his way out.

"It happened when I was sailing just off the coast of Typee," Uncle Frank begins, the cowlick sticking from his head as if his hair has never been combed. He always starts this way, using the deep pause after the first line to pull him down into the depths of the story. He stares into a space somewhere above us, as we wait eagerly for the next line. "I was a boy who thought he was a man," he says. "But I didn't know a thing. In order to learn I had to be swallowed whole."

"Frank, you son- of-a- bitch," Uncle Robert says. "You were never a sailor, and you certainly never spent any time in the belly of a whale." Even though he's heard each story a hundred times, Uncle Robert always gets riled up. As if on cue, Uncle Frank sits back in his chair, looking like a two-year-old that's been told off. He sits silently until we scream for him to finish his story. He seems so hurt that I wonder whether he really is telling the truth. Then, he begins again.

"There's never been a whale as big as this one," Uncle Frank whispers from the rocking chair, his face aglow with the magic of his own story. "Swallowed the ship in one gulp."

Uncle Robert rises abruptly, making a lot of noise as he puts his accordion back in its case, then, after pacing the room a few times, settles back in his chair to hear the rest of the story.

It happens the same way every Sunday.

I rise from bed and stand at the window, looking for Mother. Monday is washing day. She's tracking through snow to the well. The sound of each flake as it lands upon the window, a tinkling, like a miniature bell made of glass, surprises me.

I dress quickly and quietly, not wanting to wake the others. Catherine curls in a ball now to stay warm, the blanket clenched about her. Henry scratches himself, a sign that he will soon be up. And then there's the hard sound of Eli's breathing, as if he must fight for each breath and yet can never get enough.

We each have two pairs of clothes, Uncle Frank and Uncle Robert's overalls included. So, I go about gathering the clothing worn the previous week, carrying them all in my arms, stopping in the middle of the stairway. I don't know why I like it there so much, but I stop every time I go up or down. Stop and feel the way in which the darkness in the narrow stairway intensifies the sounds of the house. The scraping and sloshing of Mother's kitchen rags against the scrub board. The deep sigh Uncle Robert makes after finishing his cup of coffee. Uncle Frank's spitting into his hand and rubbing down the cowlick in the vain hope it might actually keep. In the stairway, here, at the center of the house, it's as if I can be in all places at once, and the sound takes me there.

I make any excuse I can to go outside. Help Uncle Robert roll the beer barrels through the snow into the tavern. Help Uncle Frank in the shed with whatever new idea he has to make things work better. Bring in more water for the wash. As it turns out, I'm chopping wood out back most of the morning, and I'm happy to do it because I lose myself in the cycle of each crack of the axe blade. The snow still falls, but the tinkling sound is gone. Outside, the hush silences the bustling within the house, even muffling Uncle Frank's tinkering in the shed. Perhaps that's why I don't hear Father's approach, why the whine of the front door, the groan of the floorboards escape me.

I drop the last pile of logs in the tavern's woodhouse, and Uncle Robert's grumbling breaks the silence. If lunch is not ready at noon, he gets a headache that won't leave him until the next day. So, I enter through the back door and make my way to the kitchen through the living room. I almost don't hear the barbed voice pulling up memory like a catfish, the dark whisper that slips beneath the cookie room door. I call it the cookie room because Mother stores the cookies in there at Christmas time, but it's really just a big closet. At first, I don't recognize the voice. I can't make out the words, though I feel the weight of its swollen mouth, the curled force of its tongue.

I step closer until I stand, frozen, before the door. For a moment, the child who is me thinks that it's Santa, for every year just before Christmas, Mother and Santa have conversations in the locked living room before they let the children in to find the cookies and to see Santa's boots disappear through the back door. But as soon as the thought enters my mind, it is gone.

I wonder why she doesn't say anything. I hear her in the silence smothered by his sour breath. I hear her in the body sinking beneath the earth spilling from his mouth. I reach for the door handle but my hand is stopped by the crooked moan within. My mouth is dry, drier than the tasteless ash of his, the ash that deadens my mother's own moist lips. Again a moan like laughter, but not. I steel myself for the song of his presence, for the silence of it and the emptiness.

I open the door.

At night as Catherine curls herself against me, I kick away the thoughts of Mother's face pressed against the closet wall, the hollowness of eyes choked by acceptance. I slap at the slanted image of my father drowned in a need I can only guess at. His bare and hairy legs trembling and spent.

Mother put her finger to her lips, but there's no need. I won't say a thing. I wrap my arms about Catherine, hold her tight. I whisper to her as she sleeps. A voice as far from ashes as I can find. I tell her that the snow falling outside is an incantation, a magic that keeps us whole. I tell her that sometimes we step outside that magic, and we don't even know it. And I vow to her if she ever steps outside of it, I will always guide her home.

MAD MEG
NARRATOR | *Colorado*

Kids too short to hold a drill, or men too old to pound one, carried the rock to a pine bucket that traveled up the airshaft connecting the upper and lower drifts. The better driller you were, the lower the drift you got, the better chance to hit a vein and maybe pocket a little for yourself. With only two drifts off the main tunnel, the "Meg" was a young mine, and it needed young miners to make the twenty minute hike up the face of La Nana just to begin work there. Though, soon the miners built themselves cabins to save the trouble of making the hike, leaving the sum total of their energy for the mine.

The drill-turners were almost always children, boys who came west with their fathers lusting for the ten to forty dollars a day they could make in the mines. Often, the drillers could barely make out the outline of the drill-turner's tiny hand holding the bit. So they placed candles at chest height along the rock, and the wax dripped onto the black caps on the boys' heads but that was better than having the wax drip into their eyes. The placement of the candles, the distance of a man's outstretched hands, was crucial, partly based on the need to best light the driller's swing area, but mainly because it made it easy for the men to relight their pipes with a simple lean and nod of the head.

The candle told the driller how much room he had to swing his hammer, to drive it home on the bit. Its light defined his world, his swing area, and that space was all the world he needed. For, if a driller's hand fell outside of that world, if he hit another man with his hammer, he was moved to clean up duty in the main tunnel. Though the "main" was closest to the sunlight, to the surface, it was the worst punishment he could receive because there most of the ore had been cleared away.

Will Markey never received that punishment. It was Will who

first called the mine "Mad Meg" after the first shaft collapsed. In the morning, Will worked the lower drifts, his goose-bone pipe hanging from his mouth. By afternoon, having had his fill of the lower shafts, he made his way up through the main, picking up the ore that fell from his two mules along the way.

By evening, Will Markey stayed outside. Each day he told the men it was because he was needed to consult with Henry, which was often the case. But more often it was because the cold damp of the mine, the constant fifty-five degrees, made his bones ache. With the sixth sense miners have when it comes to weakness in rocks or in humans, they joked that Will was older than the mountain, with as many cracks and precipices, and sometimes, by the end of the day, he wondered if they were right.

Henry knew rocks, but he'd come to realize he didn't know as much as he'd thought about mining. Everything he learned in that first year, he learned from Will Markey.

Will Markey was the reason Henry didn't think of quicksilver poisoning when the horses and mules began to die. It was Will who'd supervised the two tow-haired boys who drove first the mules and then the horses through the ore, forcing them to stir up the mixture with their hooves. Six months after they began taking ore from the mine and extracting it, the mules died. The horses followed two months later, and three more months after that the two boys grew sick and were taken to Denver. What caused Henry even more trouble was that Markey didn't seem to be physically affected by the extraction process. Will Markey stood alongside those boys every step of the way. In fact, when the boys first showed signs of the sickness, he even took over for them. Yet, somehow, he'd survived. Henry couldn't figure out the problem because it had no logical reasoning behind its answer. What saved Will Markey was the fact that he never took that goose-bone pipe out of his mouth. With all the tobacco he was inhaling, he hadn't had the chance to take the quicksilver into his lungs—either that, or the strange alchemy of the mixture nullified the quicksilver's poisons. Will Markey suggested the latter explanation, but Henry couldn't understand such things.

That's why when the second shaft collapsed at the end of that first year Henry didn't understand that the best thing to do would be to close it down. Instead, he spent days plumbing its depths, searching for fault lines, for signs of future instability. He even brought specialists in from Leadville, who guaranteed him that the shaft would hold. He didn't understand that the earth treasured her mysteries, kept her inscrutable parts secreted in darkness; he didn't understand that the second shaft ran straight into the heart of the mountain, and that the mountain would fight to protect that heart.

THE FLIGHT OF THE HAWK
MEG | *Wisconsin*

Everyone thought Killian would die after the roof beam from One-Eared Louie's farm fell on him, but he didn't. He stepped to the side at the last moment. So, instead of crushing his skull, the beam just gave it a good whack. Probably not much harder than some I've given him. Even still, the doctor didn't give Killian much of a chance. So, I put Catherine in bed with the other boys. Let Killian sleep alone that week. But it didn't matter. Each morning I found her back with him.

I often wondered if it was Catherine's simple desire to lie next to her oldest brother, as she'd always done, that had made the difference and saved him. Either that or he'd inherited my own stubborn will.

What I refused to think, no matter how often it worked its way into my mind, was that some compact had been reached between my oldest and youngest, a bargain made in their shared dream, a smaller life offered up to the other; or, perhaps, knowing they could not both survive, their two spirits had joined. For the day after Killian awoke from his coma, Catherine came down with a sore throat, followed by headache and fever. At first I didn't think anything of it. Having just escaped one tragedy, it was impossible to conceive of another. I assumed she had a cold or, at worst, the flu. Even Doctor Apfelbeck was hesitant to give voice to the growing suspicion inside him.

Killian first mentioned the nature of her illness to me, and the fact that she would die. Since waking from his coma, he'd taken to rising even earlier than usual and walking along the river before dawn. I could see him out there sometimes beyond the elms, watching the hawks circling, searching for their first meal of the day. I'd call him to come in, but he wouldn't listen. And I got to wondering if the beam had made him deaf and dumb.

"Catherine's got polio," he'd said. "She's going to die at the end of the month."

I slapped him. For that I can never forgive myself.

Four days later, she lost movement in her right leg and was beginning to have trouble breathing. We brought the doctor in, but besides giving a name to what we already knew, he could do little. Killian stayed with his sister throughout the day, playing games with her until she grew tired, and I watched over her throughout the night. Some evenings, Frank and Robert stepped in, sitting with Catherine, Robert playing his accordion, making up songs that made her smile, while Frank told his stories.

"When the whale swallowed me, I thought I was dead for sure," Frank would say, sitting on the wood stool beside the bed.

At first I didn't want him filling her with fancies. Why tell lies to a suffering child? But then I saw the power of those stories, the way Catherine looked at him, as if she'd shut out the rest of the world, even me. It's hard for a mother to feel that she's not part of her child's world, but in this case, I was happy for it.

He'd sit beside her like that telling his stories for hours as I looked on. Even at three years old, Catherine knew what he was doing. But she didn't mind; she loved the stories. And no matter how much he mixed them up, they all ended the same. "I learned one thing while trapped in the darkness," he would lean in close, whispering in her ear. "You've got to believe in something. That's what makes the world magic. I always believed I would escape and sure enough I did."

On the eighth day, Frank leaned in close to repeat the words Catherine had learned to recite herself, but this time the little girl turned to him. "I'm going to die tomorrow," she said in between breaths. "I believe it. Does that make it magic?"

Only the odd slant of Frank's smile gave away his surprise. He hadn't meant for her to take his words that way. At first, he didn't know how to respond. Neither did I. A mother should never hear those words from her child's lips.

I think Frank had seen death as the dark belly from which Catherine had to be delivered, that's why he'd told her the stories, or maybe that's what I wanted to believe, the reason I sat in the corner and listened. She'd seen more clearly. She'd understood that it was this world that was the dark one, the shadow, and her belief would carry her from it.

I didn't care. I would not lose her from any world. I called for the doctor, hitched the team for the trip to Milwaukee. They had a hospital there. But when everything was ready, when I'd heated the rocks for the sleigh and brought the furs to bundle Catherine in, she stopped me with one look from her wide, brown eyes. I fell to the floor beside the bed, covering my ears.

"I don't want to go to the hospital," she'd said, her words so soft that I prayed I'd imagined them. "I want to die here."

I shut the door to the room then. Climbed in bed with her and laid her head in the crook of my arm, wrapping the blankets about us. I heard myself talking to her all the while, knowing even then, the purpose of the talk was to calm me.

"Why do people assume adults are stronger than children?" I asked her.

She smiled.

"Physical strength is nothing, is it?" I asked.

She said nothing. She didn't need to.

I don't know how long I sat there before Killian opened the door, staring at the both of us in bed, a look of wonder upon his face.

"What is it?" I asked him.

"A great bird," he said. "A hawk, I think. But it's shimmering." He held a hand out as if to touch it. "It's whispering something to you," he said. Then, he dropped his hand to his side and turned and ran through the door, out into the yard, and down the line of elms.

I sat up in the bed, willing myself to move further, but found I could not. How often since I've wished I could have felt the fragile grace of her bird breath upon my skin. How different things might have been if I'd have heard her words or even the twitter of her voice in my ear. How, perhaps, I could have been there for Killian and the other boys if I'd just felt her downy arms about me once more.

THE TREE OF LIFE
KILLIAN | *Colorado*

Elizabeth presses her legs together and clenches her teeth, digs her heels into the bed sheets until I think Henry Jr. will have to cut his way out if he wants to see the world.

"Take a leg and hold it," Jess Carter says, taking a hold of one of Elizabeth's legs herself. "And don't let her close them. This baby's coming."

Jess Carter doesn't live in Seven Falls. She's been acting as midwife around the county for several years now, and came all the way from Montezuma to help Elizabeth birth the baby.

"I want you to start pushing," Jess says, nodding for me to put a warm cloth on Elizabeth's forehead. "The baby's dropped. It's time." Elizabeth gazes at her as if from far away, her eyes wild like she's lost in a snowdrift and doesn't know which way to dig. Jess gives me a look that asks if she can count on me. And I swear her red hair looks like it bursts into flame.

Elizabeth props herself up on her hands and pushes. And though the spring snow still covers the ground out back, sweat beads her forehead. "I can't do it!" She screams even as she pushes harder. "It's tearing me apart!"

"I can see the head," I shout, surprised. "The hair's black!"

Elizabeth arches her back, as she lets out a long, low, animal groan.

"He's crowning, Elizabeth," Jess says, taking a clean towel in her hands to receive the baby.

The head slowly forces its way, blood and a yellowish liquid squirting out alongside it, forced by the pressure. The face is blue, scrunched tight against the light of the new world. As it's emerging, the head turns as if taking in its surroundings, though the eyes are still closed. Then, like a great stone set in place, the head stops.

Jess gives me that look again, this time not asking but demanding

I be ready, then says to Elizabeth, "You're going to need to push even harder now."

Elizabeth shoots her a puzzled look.

"Are you listening to me, Elizabeth," Jess goes on in the same sure tone. "The baby is stuck. Now I want you to push again, and I want you to push as hard as you can, as if everything else was just a warm up."

Elizabeth nods her head, takes a deep breath then pushes, screaming this time so that the whole town must hear her. But the baby's head remains where it is. Eyes shut. Skin going purple.

Downstairs, the pine floorboards creak under Henry's steps. An owl hoots outside the bedroom window, and I wonder if it's a good omen or a bad one. I take in the room as if I'd never seen it before: the dark oak desk and dresser Henry bought in Denver, the lace curtains that were a wedding gift from Pete Myers, the row of stone jars beneath the window, jars in which Elizabeth says she keeps parts of herself (jars in which I'm afraid to look, not knowing exactly what she means), the Ute blanket hanging on the wall that Henry traded for when a nomad family passed through last fall, and the brass bed with its new satin sheets, sheets Elizabeth now lies upon, sheets she told Henry not to put on before the birth. But Henry, who has very few requirements, insists on fresh satin sheets every day, regardless of what happens to them.

"Now push!" Jess shouts and Elizabeth responds.

The baby's face remains unchanged.

"Killian," Jess shouts. "It's time!" And without a word or even understanding what I'm doing I follow the midwife's actions, helping her as she turns Elizabeth over onto all fours, the baby's head now sticking out the back, like some dark and stone-faced twin. And then Jess goes to work, sticking one hand up the swollen opening, in alongside the baby, and the other hand up Elizabeth's other hole, both hands working in unison, delicately pushing on the baby, rotating it, then putting pressure again, working the baby loose. "Push, Elizabeth!"

I no longer know what it is that the midwife pulls from her body.

"Get the moss to stem the bleeding," Jess shouts to me, and I leap across the room and back, carrying two handfuls. She is already slicing through the cord with a knife I hadn't seen, and when she is done, she hands me the baby, exchanging it for the moss. "Cover it and take it outside," she says. "Quickly! The shock of cold air will help it to breathe." Forgetting that Jess set aside clean blankets, I tear the Ute blanket from the wall and run down the stairs.

"And rub the baby under the blanket," she yells after me. "Up toward the heart."

Henry runs passed me on the stairs, unaware I carry his child in my arms.

My feet break through the frozen snow, as I run behind the house. My only thought is to be near the river, and that's where I stop. I adjust the blanket around the baby and gaze down into its chiseled-shut eyes. Not knowing what to do, I prod it under the arms with my finger.

The owl calls again from above. I search the branches over my head and see nothing. And then all at once two large, golden eyes that become my world entire. *Not now!* I shout to the owl. *I'm needed here.* I force myself out of the owl's eyes until I see it whole. And there in the owl's beak is a field mouse, freshly killed.

"Baby," I say, turning my gaze to the being in my arms, for I still do not know if it's a boy or a girl. "It's time to enter this world." And then I wiggle my hand beneath the blanket and begin massaging the baby with two fingers, pushing the blood upward.

The owl fixes me with its gaze.

I forget the way Mother's skull pushed out from her face.

I forget the dark absence of Father's gray eyes.

I forget the sound of my own voice.

Only the music floating through the rafters, vibrating the near-perfect web. And the spider, waiting.

The baby cries out.

I return only to see Elizabeth's face contort with the pain of the second set of contractions.

"Oh God," she says. "I can't make it through another one."

"This second birth is not as bad," Jess replies. "You'll make it." And sure enough with a few small pushes this round, bloody bag squishes out onto the bed, the cord attached to it still pulsing with life. It looks to me like a horse's stomach I saw once when One-Eared Louie had to put down Sam, his best workhorse. One-Eared Louie prided himself on wasting nothing, and he took me aside that day and showed me the horse's viscera as he gutted it and dried the meat.

But then Jess takes the afterbirth up in her hands and gently places it in a bucket filled with fresh water and begins to scrub it clean, only her actions are more like a caress, a holy sacrament than any type of scrubbing. She washes away the blood, and from my position at the foot of the bed I can already see the shimmering whiteness beneath.

Jess takes it from the water and holds it as if it were a baby, then brings it to the bed and sits beside Elizabeth, who gestures me to sit alongside her. I hand the baby to Henry, who takes it awkwardly. Jess holds the afterbirth before us so we can get a good look, then proceeds to tell us of the tree of life, the blue vein running from the cord up through the center of it, a vein stronger and clearer than any vein of silver ore Henry ever found in the mountain.

It starts with the pulsing cord, and I reach out and take it in my hand, right there at the base, to see if the pulsing life running through it is real. I feel it as I feel my own beating heart, wondering at the force that drives it. It's then Jess takes my hand in hers and guides my finger as it traces the pulse to its source. I follow the trunk through its infinite branches, and I feel the pulses as if they were singing in the branches of my brain. Outlined before me, the tree stands greater than any elm or oak I've ever seen.

TOAD
KILLIAN | *Wisconsin*

The toad is about four inches long and the color of dirt that has not seen rain. When I'm not standing beside Catherine's bed, watching her breathe, I'm down behind the shed studying the spots and swirls of brick red on the toad's back. The almost orange stripe down the middle. The dark throat that scares me the way it puffs out, reminding me of Catherine's breathing. It's there in the same place every day, and every day it looks the same.

When I stare at the colors, the patterns of spots, of warts long enough, things start shifting. My head spins until I feel as if I'm rising above the world. I gaze down at the shed, the apple tree and the elms that line the road, the fields beyond and smile at how funny it seems, the way everything curves and bends, how the colors stretch out before me.

My arms stretch to the ground, and I rub the toad's back with the tip of my finger. The cool wetness of its skin, the way my finger just glides over it, even over the spots, makes me happy. Now Catherine's sick. She can't get out of bed and run her fingers along its cool back.

When I let go of the toad, it hops away. I dive after it, catch its back leg as it tries to get away. Holding the toad tightly, I run into the shed, to the corner where Father piles the old coffee cans. Gently, I set the toad on the ground in the musty dark of the shed and quickly cover it with a can. "Can't get away now," I tell it, then go in to see Catherine to tell her that the toad is safe, waiting for her beneath the can.

That afternoon I lie beside Catherine, curl against her on the bed. Uncle Robert and Uncle Frank are busy in town, and Mother is resting, so Catherine and I are alone. She smells different this afternoon. I wonder if it's like the shift in the color of the sky, the result of staring at the spots on the toad too long. I don't like the smell; it reminds me of when Eli buried me in the leaves we'd raked last month. It'd rained the day before and the leaves smelled like the back of the cellar. When I cried, Eli sat on the pile and wouldn't let me out.

I want to tell Catherine that I don't like the smell. I want to ask her if she can please go back to the way she used to be. Mother says Catherine always smells like moonlight, but that's not it at all—she smells like Catherine, and that's what I want her to be. But I don't ask her to try to go back, because she needs all her strength, and I wouldn't want her to strain herself doing something that's no use. Her body's changing, and she can only watch and wait. So, I tell her about the toad, that it's waiting for her, too.

Later, I go back to check on the toad. I'm going to bring it to Catherine, so she can touch it. But when I lift the coffee can, the toad looks strange under the lamplight, not right at all. I squat down before it, peering in close at the dried out husk on the ground. I touch it, hesitantly at first, but then I push at it with my finger, try and get it to move. The spots of red, the orange stripe are gone, all turned to a gray mud.

"That's not my toad," I cry, and I back away.

I want to tell Catherine. But Mother sits upon Catherine's bed, and Catherine is holding her. She has long arms that wrap all the way around, keeping Mother warm. Catherine's lips are pressed to Mother's ear, as if she's whispering something to her, as if her whisper is a kiss. She shimmers in the light, and I wonder if this is where my toad's colors went. Then, Catherine is gone, and I run out the door to follow her until she's lost through the tops of the trees.

I don't come back at all that day. At night, I sleep along the riverbank, staring at the moon and the stars. The way they move in the sky. But no matter how much they move, I can still find my favorites, the ones Uncle Frank named after the whale that ate him, or the bear that held him in its cave, or the great oak that swallowed him whole only to belch him out the next day. Like the stories, Uncle Frank never changes; he comes out of whatever gobbled him up looking and smelling the same as he was when he went in.

The next day I make my way home, stopping on the front porch to study the movement of the clouds as they pass over. There are noises inside the house—murmuring voices—and I don't want to listen. I only want to watch and wait like Catherine does. So, that's where Mother finds me, wrapping her arms about me in the same way Catherine held her. Saturdays fresh bread and cinnamon; Sundays incense from church; Mondays lye from washing the clothes; Tuesdays ammonia and bleaching powder from cleaning; Wednesdays pears and peaches; Thursdays raspberries, which she picks for Friday's pies—and the smell of dandelions—which is always a mystery; Fridays chickens for the one night of the week the tavern offers a home cooked meal, and it takes until halfway through Saturday's baking to get rid of the smell.

I inhale her, but where I expect to smell raspberries, I smell again the cellar smell of musty leaves. Mother takes me by the hand and leads me inside where the family is gathered along with lots of people from the town: Judge Salt, Doctor Apfelbech, Mr. and Mrs. Kepsky, the schoolteacher, Miss Hull, Bert Allar, Mr. and Mrs. Lukowicz, Jake, and many others.

There's a pine box in our living room where the Christmas tree used to be, the same tree Catherine and I trimmed with popcorn and candles. I let go of mother's hand and look inside the box. I want to touch the thing that lies there, run my hand along its skin, but they tell me to keep my hands away. They tell me it's Catherine, that's what they say, my family and the townspeople who come to visit, who stand for a while in front of the box, then turn to each other with torn faces and long arms to hold. No, she doesn't smell like moonlight. She doesn't smell like Father's furs either. I don't know what it is that remains behind, and I never was able to follow Catherine past the elms. She simply faded away. So, I reach inside the box anyway, stretching my arm so I can run my finger along the bridge of her nose, then over her lips and down her neck. She doesn't feel the same either.

I want to give her something, to put something under her pillow the way Uncle Frank does sometimes, when he wants to surprise us. But the only thing I have is the stub of my pencil from school. So I slide that under her pillow when no one is looking.

I step outside. The sky is blue again, the sun yellow. I decide I like the other colors better, the ones that came after staring at the toad, the ones Catherine seemed to take on after she flew from her bed; they seemed more real.

THE CAMP
NARRATOR | *Colorado*

Silas Cordley stumbled half-groggy with sleep through the sun-bled pines. The wood sap stuck to his hand, and he tried to suck it off. And in this way, he walked smack into a web hanging between the branches of the diseased lodgepole that shaded Fitch Wise's tent. He jumped back, swatting at the web. "Goddamn it!" he said, brushing the strands from his shoulder. He imagined the spider crawling up his neck and arched his head back to see. Behind him, the preacher, Wilbert Marshall, sat on a large rock watching him. They stared at each other without saying anything. Wilbert took a long swig from his bottle.

"Shut up," Silas said, finally.

Wilbert tucked the bottle in his jacket, pulling the jacket tight about him. His gaze fixed on Silas.

Silas turned toward the tent, crouching lower than he needed to beneath the branches of the pine. "Fitch, you lazy Englishman, wake up!" he shouted.

"Look at me," Wilbert mumbled to himself.

Silas ignored him.

"It's come to me now," Wilbert went on.

"Shut up!" Silas shouted over his shoulder, then knelt before the tent. "Fitch, wake up. You missed breakfast, and I need your help working the long tom."

"I ain't real," Wilbert said. "We ain't none of us more than a shadow blown over the dirt."

Silas turned his attention to the drunk preacher who sat on the rock scratching himself. "Why don't you tell it to Fitch," Silas said. "You're making my head hurt." A faint tickle climbed his neck, worked its way into his hair, not the spider but its ghost. "Goddamn it!" he said again, brushing at his neck, running his hands through his hair. Then, he pulled back the tent flap and peered inside.

"Lord, part the heavens and come down. Touch the mountains until they pour forth smoke," Wilbert shouted, standing now upon the rock. "Send Your lightning, Your arrows, so that I might feel what it means to be alive."

"Son of a bitch!" Silas shouted, closing the tent flap. "Son of a bitch!"

Will Markey tried to break up the fight, but Big Jim Leek had been eyeing Fitch's tent for a long time and Tom Thomas, or Double Tom as they liked to call him, jumped the claim before Fitch's body had even been removed, placing his things inside, tossing those of Fitch's out, at least the ones he didn't want.

Big Jim thought he'd use his size to intimidate Double Tom, who was short but stocky. When Double Tom emerged from the tent to go for the last of his supplies, Big Jim simply stood in his way.

By the time Will Markey arrived, the other miners had circled the two men, some cheering for Big Jim (who was a hard worker and thus had earned the miner's respect, but also simply because they were afraid of him), and some choosing the underdog (who though he often appeared mean-spirited had proven his heart on many occasions when a miner needed tobacco or was temporarily short of food). It was the greedy speed with which Double Tom had taken over Fitch's tent, working against his otherwise generous reputation, that had the miners talking while the two men fought. And Double Tom had taken a pretty fair beating, though like a badger he kept coming back for more, when Will Markey stood between the two, blowing great clouds of smoke from his goose-bone pipe.

"I'm not living by the shit hole any more," Double Tom said, wiping his mouth with his shirt in a vain attempt to make himself appear more civilized. "This camp stinks straight to hell, and I've had to live by the patch of dirt you all call a toilet for too long." A few miners nodded, as if in agreement, while others whose tents were farther away set their jaws hard, thinking Double Tom was a whiner and that any man should be able to put up with a little bad smell. Will Markey puffed on his pipe, thinking of the judgment he would proclaim.

"I'm not staying where I am, Will," Double Tom pleaded.

"I just done what—"

"Shut up!" Will Markey said. "You think you got a say in this? You think it matters how you came to this point? It don't matter at all."

"What are you talking about, Will?" Double Tom said, spitting blood. A trickle of red saliva dribbled on his shirt. "I found it first."

"You think Fitch reckoned he had a say?" Will Markey asked. The men went silent. Even Double Tom wiped the toothless grin from his face. "Besides, we've got another problem," Will Markey said. "One the rest of you brainless heathens failed to notice."

"What's that, Will?" various voices from the crowd asked.

"It seems Fitch here has been murdered, his head nearly lopped off in his sleep," Will Markey took the goose-bone pipe from his mouth. "And my guess is that one of you did it."

The miners looked one to another, all except Wilbert Marshall who was now sleeping on the rock. Will Markey refilled his pipe and took his time lighting it.

Silas Cordley stood silent in the center of the crowd, hoping another would give voice to his thoughts. Then that voice came. "But Will," it said. "Fitch is already dead and gone. What good's it going to do now to keep a man from working in the mine, especially when that man might be the one to find the mother lode? We're all in this together, Will."

Will Markey kept on puffing, until, one by one, the men dispersed. Alone, he looked over the mess of Fitch's things that Double Tom had tossed on the side of the tent, then, without so much as a glance in either direction, he bent down and pulled himself a good pair of working boots from the pile and walked away.

THE LANGUAGE OF SELF
HENRY | *Wisconsin*

I talked to his back. No matter if I started speaking to his front I would end speaking to his back. I soon learned that his back understood better than his front, that his back heard all it needed to from me. Still, I remember wondering if my words made sense, or if perhaps I was speaking a different language, one he couldn't understand. Killian and Eli never went with him for that reason, at least that's what Killian said. He said he couldn't find the words, he said that when he spoke Father scarcely looked in his direction at all. Like them, I was going to give up, though I hated quitting anything. It's not in me. But then I realized that Father was also trying to speak with me, and if I wanted his love I must learn his alphabet. And so I followed, ears attuned in ways only a child understands, to the subtle straightening that signaled approval, the droop that indicated disgust, or the curve in the spine that said to be quiet.

I followed him out the door and down the line of elms in the kind of cold dark that only comes on an October morning when you are not quite yet expecting it, the kind of morning where the frost washes over everything, and you feel that the world as you know it has been buried, covered over. I remember wanting to stop and touch the hoarfrost on the grass, to marvel at the beauty of its crystalline structure, but not daring to for fear I would miss a telltale sign from his back.

He stood so tall before me, my father. I spent the first hour watching him, the way his head draped in coonskin blotted out the sky. His back seemed so wide I could scarcely imagine learning the entirety of its language. I remember thinking there were simply too many words, too many rules for an eight-year-old to fathom.

He kept his Springfield tucked tight under his arm, barrel pointed to the ground before him, so that learning the myriad positions of the rifle's butt end beneath his arm was also part of my study of vocabulary. Held close and tight to his armpit meant it would be a long march to the hunting ground, and I best keep up for he would not wait. Held low and loose meant he was in good humor and, perhaps, I could stop for a moment to examine a glistening stone along the path or even an arrowhead under my foot. Once when I saw his rifle hanging in the crook of his arm I ventured to walk beside him for a spell. He turned to me, sparing a smile out of the left corner of his mouth. Frightened because I could not understand the particular diction of that smile, I fell in behind him once again.

The first shot echoed as the bronze sun peered over the horizon, bringing little warmth. The pheasant dropped before it was twenty feet in the air. I jumped when it burst from the cattails and weeds before us along with two other birds. My breath caught as it thrust itself into the sun, all wings and neck. And then it was gone. Father took the bird by the neck, tied a noose around it and strung it to his belt. He asked if I wanted to see, but I kept my distance. The frosted ground seeped through my boots, creeping into my bones, and I remember having to hold myself to keep warm. I told my father I had to pee and went off behind a cottonwood. I stayed there as long as I thought it safe to remain, as long as I could before he came looking for me.

One by one, he took the birds he'd shot and strung them to his belt, so that soon there were six dangling from his waist. With each, the smell of death increased upon my father—the smell of all things cold: steel, stones, and decay—and with each I seemed to fall farther and farther behind him, until with the last, the bird fell from the sky before the gun fired.

Without a word, my father turned, heading back the way we came. I knew he'd had his fill for the day. As he approached, he grew larger and larger, or I grew smaller and smaller. I'm not sure which. All I remember was that as he passed I felt sure the creature that walked by was a giant risen from the muddy earth and not my father at all. If I had not relieved myself already, I surely would have wet my pants.

The sun was still only halfway to its zenith, its light not yet bringing the warmth I so desired, and all I could think about was the comfort of home. For that reason, I stayed a pace behind my father, matching him stride for stride, even as his own pace increased. He held the Springfield in his hand now, something he only did when he was in a hurry, when he wanted nothing to get in his way. And so I said nothing, but followed, fearing he was trying to lose me, to leave the boy who, like his others, had so clearly already failed him.

And then he stopped and brought the rifle to sight. Following the line of his aim, I tried to locate his prey. For I understood my father well enough to know that it must be a special prey to cause him to change his plan. I remember in that brief instant scanning the horizon for a bear or a cougar—even though I knew there were no cougars, at least not in Wisconsin. But I think I wanted there to be some such animal. I think I needed there to be something grand, something out of the ordinary to save what I knew had already become of this day. Even when I saw the squirrel in the treetop for the second before it fell, I thought it was some strange creature from a dream, a new species never before discovered at the very least.

Stunned, I stood staring at the lifeless body of the squirrel upon the ground. Only when the echo of the rifle's discharge faded did I try to speak, yet no words came. My father sat upon a log and gestured for me to bring the squirrel to him.

I stood rooted to the ground, no longer frozen as I'd been before, but because I was actually weighing in my mind whether or not to obey him. And then I walked toward the dead animal. I wonder now why my father had the patience at that moment, when he normally wouldn't have waited two seconds for me. But he waited what must have been a very long time, as I carefully approached the squirrel. The smell hit me first, the same smell given off by the pheasants tied to my father's waist, a smell that chilled much more than the air that was now, finally, turning warm.

I kneeled down before the squirrel, staring into its black, lifeless eyes, then turned toward my father and stared into his own gray eyes. I thought I had learned his language, but no matter how hard I tried to see into him, I could not understand.

My father met my gaze, gesturing with his hand for me to pick up the dead animal.

I turned again toward the squirrel, my eyes now fixed on the gaping hole in its side, the blood pooling there. I reached out my hand but could not bring myself to grab it. I must admit now I was partly afraid the thing would come alive again and bite me, but it was also the sense that something gravely wrong had occurred and that no matter what my action was I could not change it.

I must have been kneeling there with my hand inches from the squirrel for a very long time because my father appeared suddenly at my side, dropping his handkerchief at my feet.
He thinks I'm afraid, I thought, afraid to stain myself with the blood. I was angry with him for that, and still I took the handkerchief from him, spread it over the squirrel so that I wouldn't have to see it, picked it up, and handed it to him. He took it in his own hands, placed it before me, and opened the handkerchief.

"Look, Henry," he said.

I kept my face averted.

"Look," he said again. "Look closely."

Slowly, I turned my gaze upon it.

"This is death," he said. "It doesn't mean a thing." Then he clenched the animal in his fist and threw it into the bushes, pocketing the bloody handkerchief after.

I followed my father the rest of the way home, but I no longer studied his back. Understanding was an impossibility. Instead, I kept my gaze upon the ground, scouring the dirt and rocks for a new language, one that would be my own. That search would take me the rest of my life, but I have found it, and it has given me much comfort. Though I have realized only too late, that, like my father, I have enclosed myself in my own dialect, one that is difficult for anyone else to learn. I don't know why it is that in order to find ourselves we must so often lose that very self to others.

THE MESMERIST
KILLIAN | Colorado

The mesmerist must have slipped into town sometime during the drizzly night, setting up his tent before dawn. Webb would have already gotten up as the mesmerist pounded in the last stake, he would have finished feeding at Elizabeth's breast as the mesmerist put on his flowing multi-colored robe, and he would have been playing on the floor beside Elizabeth's bed while the mesmerist took a dram of whiskey then hid the bottle in the Chinese cabinet in the private room in the back of his tent.

Scarcely able to see in the darkness, which creeps away so slowly these autumn mornings, I enter Elizabeth's room, searching for the cooing shape upon the floor that is Webb. Finding it, I scoop him up and bound out of the room so that he doesn't even have time to squeal. Not that it would matter, as Elizabeth will sleep the day away, turning her back to him if he enters the room, only offering her breast if told to by Henry or myself. Webb turned a year last month and gets by just fine on the food we give him.

Together, Webb and I creep into Henry Jr.'s room. I let Webb crawl over Henry Jr.'s face to wake him up. Henry Jr. doesn't mind; he loves his brother, and most of all he loves the walks we take each morning before school on school days and all morning long on Saturdays and Sundays. Today is Saturday. It doesn't matter that it's raining this morning. We'll even go out in the snow once that comes, and I can tell by the crisp morning air, the way it bites back at you when you try to take a breath, that the snow's coming soon.

"Where are we going this morning, Uncle Killian?" Henry Jr. asks as he pulls his pants up over his long johns.

"Didn't you hear that hammering this morning?" I ask, leading them downstairs, ransacking the pantry for food. Henry takes his meals in town or at the mine, and Elizabeth generally doesn't eat, so finding anything for the children is difficult.

"I thought that sound was the miners," Henry Jr. replies, his eyes widening as he realizes his growling stomach may have to wait.

"Can't you tell the difference?" I ask. "The miners' hammering is muffled, running down through the rock to us from the mountain, but this hammering's sharp, higher pitched; it's right here in town."

Frost sparkles in the frozen mud of Main Street, mud that thaws up just enough to cover your shoes by noon and right over your ankles by two. Mud that will be frozen again by sundown. Henry Jr. is fascinated, stopping often to touch the hoary white, prying a pinch loose to bring it to his tongue, while Webb eyes me from inside my coat, content to look upon my face and stay warm. We walk toward the east end of town, away from the three mountains hovering over our backs, but I feel the trees upon those mountains blazing in the new morning sun, calling me, willing me to wander and lose myself in those hills, as I so often do.

The tent is red and bigger than any I've ever seen. Uncle Robert's voice echoes in my head, what he would say every time Uncle Frank told us of the size of the whale that swallowed him: "Anything bigger than your head, Frank, is certainly not of this world, of that I'm sure!" I call to Henry Jr. as he runs to the tent, but he pays me no mind, and so I run along after him, Webb bouncing in my coat.

A large sign fronts the tent, showing a man dressed in a long, flowing robe of every imaginable color. The man stands over a woman in a dark blue dress, who is seated in a chair. She looks strange, this woman. Different from any of the women in town. And it's not because she's an Indian; rather it's the way she stares out of the picture. The man in the colorful coat is passing some sort of stick or wand over her head, and the Indian woman stares out like she sees right through the man, right through us all. It makes my skin shiver. Wavy lines stretch out from the stick and run straight into the woman's head. I can't read the words under the picture, but I want to know what those lines are doing. They look just like the trees that blaze in my mind.

Just then, a man emerges, appearing identical in every way to the man in the poster, except he has a thick black beard. "Mesmerism," he says. "The science of the future brought to your sleepy little town today, courtesy of Wellington Taylor." And with that the man extends his gem-covered hand.

I take it in my own, watching to see if any wavy lines come out of it, wondering if he can control the lines, or if, like me, he opens to the fire whenever and wherever it appears. The man looks at me with a queer eye, murmuring beneath his breath, then grips my hand harder like he wants to pull me into the tent right then and there.

"First show's at one o'clock," the man says. "If you have an interest in the modern sciences, I suggest you attend."

We spend the morning on the porch of Pete Myers' General Store, and he gives us breakfast along with some licorice if we keep the dogs off his produce. Everyone that comes into the store talks about the mesmerist. "They say he trained with an Englishman," Lulu Giberson says as she picks up a sack of potatoes and another of onions. "I hear he's royalty," Tom Guller says, taking a break from cleaning out his saloon.

By noon, the entire town is standing nearly ankle deep in the mud, waiting for the mysterious stranger to open the flaps to his tent and invite them inside. It's warm enough now, so I take Webb out of my coat, and we join the crowd. Webb points to the tent, screaming something I don't understand. The woman must have come out when I wasn't looking or I would have seen her. She's shorter than in the picture, and her skin has such deep lines that I wonder if she's real. Her eyes are the color of her black hair and with the same thickness, like they go on and on. The crowd gasps at the sight of her, and I hear a few voices say, *She's an Indian, a Ute to be sure.* I've never seen an Indian in person, but I've heard tales of Ute camps out beyond the Blue.

"Ten cents," the Ute woman says, and I don't know if it's because I'm surprised she speaks English or because her skin is so dark and furrowed, but I don't see her mouth move as she speaks.

She sticks out her hand, and, one by one, the townspeople pay their money to enter the tent. When Frank Foote, the last of the townspeople, enters, I turn to go. Although Henry and Elizabeth have plenty of money, I've never seen the use of it until now, and don't have any money on me.

"You go free," the Ute woman says. "The children too."

I smile, take Henry Jr.'s hand, and, holding Webb in my other hand, pull back the tent flap. When I look again, the Ute woman is gone.

The inside of the tent smells like the candy jars that line the back counter of Pete Myers' store, all licorice and peppermint. And curtains hang along the sides of the tent depicting strange scenes. The one closest to me shows birds with baby faces rising into a starlit sky. I'm not sure why it's so black in the picture as both the sun and the full moon are out.

The crowd is thick and we're forced to stand in the back, but I'm taller than most anybody in town, so it doesn't matter to me. Henry Jr. disappears from my side, pushing through legs, dodging feet until he gets to the front of the stage. I set Webb upon my shoulders, so he has the best view in the house, and he squeals with delight.

It's then that the mesmerist emerges, looking just as I'd seen him earlier in the day, only now he's carrying some sort of metal wand. The Ute woman follows behind him, holding a tray before her with other things on it, though I can't tell what they are.

"Ladies and Gentleman," the mesmerist intones. "You are about to witness the powers of one of the world's great forces." And with that he pauses the slightest bit, then says just above a whisper: "Magnetism." The Ute woman steps forward.

"My assistant, Antoinette, will give a brief demonstration of this awesome power," the mesmerist goes on. "Indians, being closer to the earth, are natural conductors of magnetism."

The mesmerist waves the metal wand over the Indian's head in a circular motion. I look for the wavy lines but can't see them.

Maybe I'm too far away. The Indian starts to shake and then the mesmerist commands her to dance. She starts jumping around the stage, whooping and hollering. The few ladies in the audience cry out in horror. Even the men seem taken aback, like they're not used to seeing such sights.

"Stop!" the mesmerist commands, and the Ute woman stops and stands motionless, her gaze vacant as if her spirit has left behind the empty casing of her body.

"I know there are doubters among you," the mesmerist says, folding up the sleeves of his flowing robe. "There are some out there saying to themselves at this very moment that the Indian is only acting her part, that because she's my assistant what she does is not real." A few heads in the crowd nod. But I believe him. I almost shout it but then think better of it.

"I want to assure you that the powers of which I speak are just as real as the air you breathe, the ground you walk upon. For the power of magnetism comes from the earth itself. It is bound up with the earth and all living beings upon it." The mesmerist scans the crowd as he speaks, and then his eyes fix on me. "You, sir, the one with the baby upon your shoulders. Come forward."

The crowd parts, and I step toward the stage.

"Don't be shy," the mesmerist says. "Ladies and Gentlemen, I picked this man because he cares for children and children are a natural fount of magnetism."

As I step on stage, I see Henry Jr. smiling before me, proud his uncle has been chosen. I've forgotten that Webb is still on my shoulders until the mesmerist asks Lulu Giberson to hold him. Webb cries for a minute and reaches back to me until he notices Lulu's earrings and quickly becomes content.

"Do we know each other, sir?" the mesmerist asks me, then turns toward the audience, waiting for my answer.

"You're the mesmerist," I say.

The mesmerist puts his arm around me and laughs while

nodding to the audience. "That's right," he says. "I am. But had you met me before today?"

"No, sir," I answer. "I have not." The mesmerist turns to the crowd, his white teeth sparkling like Lulu's earrings.

"Antoinette," he goes on. "Please hand me the conductive fluid." And the Ute woman brings forth a vial of fluid. The mesmerist talks to the audience as he shakes out drops of the fluid over my head. "The fluid is harmless, but it will aid the magnetic waves, allowing them easier access to this gentleman's psyche."

The mesmerist steps to the front of the stage. "Now, witness the power of magnetism." Then, he walks back to me and waves the metal wand over my head again and again.

I keep looking for the wavy lines, but I don't see any. So I don't think anything is happening at first. But then I stretch my hand up to touch a snowflake, and I notice that the roof of the tent is gone. The air shimmers about me, changing shape, as if smoke or haze or steam is flowing about me until all is heavy and thick.

The snow falls, blurring the people until they are gone, and in their place stand trees, thousands of pines covered with the fresh, white flakes. And I know that everywhere it's time to sleep.

The snow buries me until I am no longer. Wisps of shadow float about me. I know these people. I am sure I know them. I am them. We are flying up like birds from the snow. It's then we see the wide scar of white down the face of La Nana. The fire inside so many trees extinguished. The wind howls down the freshly made path and carries a new smell to us, a smell we fear, a smell we remember well—the smell of death. We float closer to the ground, the syrupy air weighing upon our new wings.

We stick close to the snow, following the tracks, and then another smell is carried to us on the howling wind, the smell of a horse gone bad. We know that smell because we helped Henry put down a horse like that once. Its eyes rolling white, like it had forgotten how to live in the dream. Without the bees, the hawk, and the bear, we would forget too. We would lose our distance, our ability to sink between day and night.

We fly low, lost in the smell. The sound of the stillness overwhelms us—like bees in our head. And then the tomb opens, and we see the gaping wound, the sea of white. The tomb opens and trees groan. They bend and break.

The roan stands at the edge of the tomb, gazing into its depths. The horse takes his axe to the only tree left standing, the tree that marked the front yard of his cabin. We float about him and quietly sing. The roan gives no thought to it, or maybe he thinks our song is a trick of the wind. But his daughters come running and rest upon our wings. Death has not changed them so much. Once the tree is down, the roan carves into the bark with his hunting knife.

The night air chills. The moonlight shines upon the newly wrought fiddle in the roan's hooves. We wait for the sound of his playing, but he has no bow. It's then he takes her body in his arms. We hadn't recognized the soft, flickering scent of her, we didn't notice the spinning gold of her hair with so much death floating on the wind. We cannot see his face as he raises his hunting knife and cuts the hair from her head, but we know it's not unlike the twisted whine of the coyote. As morning arrives, he fastens the aspen colored hair to his bow and begins to play.

We rise into the night on wings made only to fly, wings unable to carry sorrow, wings unable to touch another.

We no longer know which is our real self, which our shadow. It no longer matters. Life and death fade one into the other. Like apparitions, madness and grief flicker before us and are gone. But how do we wake from this dreaming? We fear that we will always float in this gray sky, that this snow will never end.

They say I didn't wake for three months. They say that it took four men to carry me from the mesmerist's tent, that Webb wouldn't stop crying, that Henry Jr. hid the rest of the day for fear he'd be punished. They tell me that they tarred and feathered the mesmerist and ran him out of town before he put a spell on anyone else. They tell me that I talked in my sleep often, that I cried sometimes, that they had to force food down my mouth just to keep me alive.

But I don't remember anything except the white face of snow. Though I can't escape the feeling that I'm floating, that I'm not really part of anything. The problem is I don't know where or when I belong. It seems to me I've always been unfastened from this world, observing it as if through a dream. I want to reach out, to touch things, but all I grasp is the flapping of wings, the color of moonlight, and the keening of stars.

THE CLARITY OF MYSTERY
Eli | *Wisconsin*

I was sleeping under the birch far from town, the summer of my seventeenth year, when I awoke to the hound's baying. I followed the sound, until I came upon an animal hidden beneath brush so thick I'd have never seen her if it weren't for the hound.

A mare, gray as the sky. Nothing special about her, except her eyes. Eyes that watched me through labored breathing.

The hound scampered off, but I remained. I watched as first blood and mucous dripped from the mare's womb. I watched as that dark hole opened wider and wider, until I felt sure it would swallow me. I watched as a shimmering blue-white sac, a nearly translucent balloon, bubbled out, slimy and wet. Instead of popping, it got bigger and bigger until I was sure the mare was giving birth to the whale in Uncle Frank's story. I wanted to run. But the mare's eyes fixed me to that spot.

The sac flopped out, viscous and alive upon the ground.

I watched and waited. When would the mare rise and lick away the caul, tear away the fragments with its teeth so the foal could breathe? The mare's nostrils flared, open and closed, open and closed—two more dark holes to swallow me. It raised its head, but not to get up. It was summoning me. But I couldn't touch that quivering mass.

I ran through sheets of morning light as it filtered through the trees, leaves raining down upon me, crumbling beneath my feet. Yellow birch and hickory curling in on themselves at my approach, the flaming red leaves of the dogwood, maple, and oak marking my track.

The sac would burst. I knew it would. The foal would kick his way out from the inside. And I could not be there when it did.

The hound bayed, and I ran. I resisted as long as I could, until, finally, I stopped before the banks of the Big Eau Pleine. Kneeling upon the ground, I rubbed handfuls of dirt into my face, my skin, covering myself. But when I looked up, the hound stood waiting for me.

I tore open the caul, ripped it with my fingers, chewed it with my own teeth. The roan lay within, still as snow. I opened his mouth, cleared away the fluid that brought death as well as life, not conscious of the work my hands were doing, not aware of my self at all, except as I looked through the mare's eyes. I could see my head nudging the roan to rise. I could see my long blond hair, a mane falling over my shoulders, my goatee a patch of white sprouting beneath. I looked into the wildness of my own eyes and wondered why the mare had chosen me. The roan lay there, shaking off the fragments of its caul, kicking at the thick, now white, skin that kept it from the world. And still the mare eyed me.

I waited for the afterbirth, and when it didn't come, I knew the mare was in trouble. By then, the roan was on its feet, nuzzling its head against me. I led it out of the woods, the morning sun now free of the grasping branches.

I fed the roan cow's milk from One-Eared Louie's farm. Each day he seemed to grow bigger, more sure of himself. And I was his mother, I who'd never cared for anything before. Not like Killian who was always bringing animals home and taking care of them. I wouldn't let Killian care for it, even if he'd wanted to.

Killian watched me from the back porch each morning and evening when I fed the roan, when I took it for a walk down past the elms. It was like the mare watching me all over again. He never said anything, just stood there in his overalls with his hands in his pockets. I wanted to hit him for standing there, staring at me like that—like he was judging me.

When I wasn't caring for the roan, I kept it tied behind the shed. I never took him into town. Oscar Kepsky had been talking. He'd been telling people he thought the roan was his property. He said he'd found his dead mare out by the Birch groves. She must have run away to foal, he said. I'd run away too, if I had to live with Kepsky. He told people that he wanted to know where my horse came from. One day at breakfast, after I'd been caring for it for nearly four months, Father sat beside me at the cracked, oak table. Something he rarely did.

"Oscar Kepsky says you have his horse," he said. "Is that true?"

"I found him in the woods," I said. "He's not anybody's property." I couldn't look my father in the eyes. I just kept chewing on my bacon, turning my spoon through my grits.

"Oscar says that if he doesn't get his horse back, he's going to come over here and take it back," my father said, as if taking Oscar's side.

"Just let him try," I said. "If he comes over here, I'll kill him."

My father's eyes remained upon me, daring me to look into them, his stare unlike the mare's or Killian's. I couldn't see myself in it. It absorbed me, threw nothing back.

I knew he was trying to determine if I'd really do it. Let him wonder, I thought. It's time he considered me.

He rose from the table. "You're a man now," he said. "What you do is your business. But, it's just a horse. A dumb horse."

What did he know about animals? All he knew was how to skin them, how to prepare their hides to get the best price and most of all how to talk about the quality of the fur—its softness and thickness. What did he know about caring for something?

Kepsky must have come while I was at school. It was my last year, and it was a Friday so I normally would have taken the roan to the river to fish, but Miss Hull had invited Father Blanchard to teach the Bible. The stories from the Bible made me feel good, fixed in place like I knew who I was. Mother always said she couldn't get me to do much else, but I was the first one ready for church every Sunday. Those stories made me feel like I knew why things happened. Why the hound called me. Why the mare had died. Why my father rarely looked at me, and why when he did, I feared to look back.

I knew my father was in on it. He was home, and he wouldn't have let them on his land if he didn't agree with what they were doing. He wouldn't let anyone on his land unless he was in complete agreement. When I came home, I knew exactly what had happened. Kepsky had gone right up to our front door. He wouldn't have wanted to sneak around like the thief he was. He would have told my father he was taking the roan, and my father would have let him, not because he agreed with Kepsky that the horse was his property, but just to spite me because I'd dared to stand up to him, because I didn't cower like the rabbits and fox he hunted.

Father Blanchard's story that day told about how Jesus destroyed the temple, how our Lord grew angry and took away what the people desired.

That night at dinner Father studied me across the table. Everyone was quiet; they all knew what had happened, and they waited to see what I'd do. "It was nothing but a dumb horse," I said, the lie somehow giving me the courage to look at Father.

Mother untied her apron and sat beside me. "Maybe we could get another horse," she said. She'd heard Jake Mulenbach's horse was going to foal soon. "Maybe we could think about buying that one." She didn't understand. They thought I smiled because I might get another horse, but they didn't know. I smiled because for once Father thought he understood, and he was wrong. Now I was going to teach him something.

That night in the darkness of the new moon, I snuck into Father and Mother's room and crept quietly beneath their bed. But as I reached for the rifle he kept hidden there, my hand became lead, my arm a dead weight. I couldn't breathe. I lay there like that until I thought they'd buried me alive. I had to break the spell somehow, but there was only one way I knew. So, I lunged for the rifle and ran to Kepsky's. As I ran, I heard the hound baying again, and I knew this was the real reason I'd found the mare. I slipped through his fence, and there was my roan. He was happy to see me, nuzzling and sniffing, looking for milk.

I sat down on the fence beside the foal, stroking his mane. I told him the story of Jesus and the temple, so he might understand. I passed the night there with my arm around that horse, the rifle leaning against the fence. By morning, I wasn't sure I could do it. Maybe I'd just lead the roan home, I thought, and that would be it. But then I heard Kepsky stirring in his house. I grabbed the rifle, brought it to my shoulder. The roan looked at me with warm, wet eyes.

"Kepsky!" I shouted. "Come out here!"

It didn't take long. He came out scratching his behind, his overalls only half buttoned up. I turned the rifle on the roan, put the barrel to its forehead.

"You crazy son of a bitch!" Kepsky yelled.

I saw myself reflected in the roan's eyes, the same way I'd seen myself in the mare's. I turned away and pulled the trigger.

"You crazy . . . "Kepsky went for me, but it was like I wasn't myself anymore. I climbed casually over the fence, turned my back to him, and walked home. He didn't dare follow.

My father was leaving to meet with the trappers up north. He saw his rifle in my hands, the blood spattered on my face and shirt. But he didn't say anything. He wasn't afraid like Kepsky. He just knew the course of my life had been set. I was a man now, and no words would change that. He never asked for the rifle back, and I didn't give it to him.

Each day I feel those eyes on me, as if I couldn't make a move without their judgment. Each night, I'm trapped inside my own caul, trying to kick my way out. And when the roan eats away the last shred covering my face, there's nothing for me but to keep my eyes shut for fear of what I might see, the eyes that turn the world back upon itself.

I slip out at night sometimes, when the baying of the hound or the dark eyes of my dreams wake me. I take the rifle and run into the woods to the birch grove, looking for I don't know what.

Mother got sick a week after Father left. She couldn't stop

coughing, like she had to get something out of her. I decided to leave the morning I first visited her in bed. She was sleeping, but when she heard me come in, she opened her eyes. She knew my sin, and I knew it had caused her illness.

I ran far away. I took the rifle and my belongings and ran into the night without saying goodbye. But who will have me? And where can I run to where I won't hear the hound, where I won't have to endure my own image? We are punished for our sins. God is vengeful. He knows the greatest punishment is to hurt the ones you love. It's no mystery. I knew that when I shot the horse.

THE GEOGRAPHY OF THE BODY
Elizabeth | *Colorado*

I slipped myself off each night like a dress. Tugged at the shoulder straps and stepped out of my skin. It was the only way to stop from falling.

I fell away from my marriage. The roles Henry demanded showed me so many faces that were not mine. And most painful of all, I fell away from my children until all I saw in the mirror was a blur, a nothingness that made me sleep.

And so I fell into bed. Not just my bed but many beds: Tom Thomas' bed, Silas Cordley's bed, Big Jim Leek's bed, even Will Markey's bed, among others. You know where you are in a bed, the geography is easy to map, the shoreline clear, and it lies on every side. I could lie on my back, on my front, whatever they wanted of me, and all I needed to do was hold onto the edge to feel where I was. At least that's what I thought for the first year. But it's never that simple. We can enclose ourselves in an easily definable world, chart the topography of our bodies, but that doesn't mean we can see our faces any more clearly.

I stretched myself upon my belly, lay myself down before Big Jim, my head pointing north toward the icy clarity that never came. I needed to be pinned to the earth, held firm to the four corners of my known world.

Will Markey never took the goose-bone pipe from his mouth as I rolled upon my back. Instead, he took each of my thighs in his hands, spreading them gently, kneeling before me, taking the layout of my land.

"What are you doing?" I asked, though I rarely talked at all during these times. It is much easier if you don't talk.

"Same as you," he said, the pipe bobbing in his mouth. "Searching for a place to live."

I had to think about that one. If there were places inside, places that could hold others, then was it possible they could hold me, too?

Until that point, my reputation had not been hurt by my wanderings. But now I threw myself at the miners with abandon, desperate to find that hidden place. And it was during this time that the townsfolk's opinion of me changed. I was no longer the first lady, but the town whore. A special distinction in a place with so many women plying the trade already. I suppose the fact that I didn't charge for my services only boosted my reputation. It certainly did among the miners. They no longer cared that I required them to take a room in Demings' Hotel. At least the hotel had a firm mattress, they would say, which was more than could be said of the makeshift beds in their cabins and tents.

I don't know why I stuck exclusively to the miners. Perhaps because they worked for my husband. He controlled them in one way, and I suppose I wanted to control them in another. Husband and wife, we played on their two greatest follies: greed and lust. "Maybe they're the same thing," Will Markey told me one day. And when I thought about it, I had to agree. When I see their faces eyeing a dusty bag of silver ore just taken from the mountain, it's no different than when they fix one of the women in town beneath their stare. I'd seen the same look a thousand times on my savior and benefactor, Bertram Wheeler, when he walked into his bank. And I noted it when he paid his nightly visits to me. Even when it was too dark to see, the gluttony of his gaze slavered my skin.

It gave me great satisfaction to make the men look at me that way, to be the one holding the glass of water before them, the only one with the power to quench their thirst. It gave me satisfaction, but nothing more. I had no substance. I gave them what they needed, but no matter how much they gave back, no matter how much I took in, when it was over, I was an empty vessel.

It was as if their seed was barren, unable to engender anything born from dead lust the way it was. By the last year of my fall, I no longer had any excuse at all. I'd become sure there was no place deep inside in which to live, much less to hide.

I don't know what salvation kept me from dying. Perhaps it was the songs of their little deaths. The songs and the frantic struggling that preceded them worked like a drug, their juice like the strongest wine, deadening me so that I could walk the streets without care as people I once called friends turned away from me, whispering obscenities under their breath. If I couldn't see myself, it was fitting others shouldn't see me as well. Only the stranger, Wallace, pierced me with a look stronger than the most furious of Big Jim's thrusts, the sting of his gaze almost bringing me back to myself as I passed by the sheriff's office. Oh, how I longed for that look, how I both longed for it and feared it.

Henry's eyes, when they looked at me at all, had no such effect. It seemed the further I fell, the more he ignored me. At first, I knew it was because his character couldn't conceive of what I'd become. He rationalized me away. But when the evidence became all too clear, and he still didn't react, I was at a loss to understand. His face became a blur to me as well. I do not pretend to know my husband, as he pretends to know me. I used to. No longer. I've learned better. Yes, I've learned many things.

I've learned that you cannot run from gravity. It will always pull you downward. Not even a bed, not even a careful mapping of your world, an intricate study of the body's geography can save you. Gravity will win every time.

THE COLORS OF THE RIVER
KILLIAN | *Wisconsin*

"Killian, your mother's sick," Doctor Apfelbeck tells me as we stand in the fur room, pelts from Father's last trip piled high in the corner next to the piano. "It's not polio," he says. "It's not like what Catherine had. This disease is going to be with her for a long time."

"Uncle Robert says she's got consumption," I reply. "Is that true?"

"You're her oldest," Doctor Apfelbeck continues, not saying whether it's true or not, but looking at me with eyes that want to tell me something, something he can't say with his mouth. "She's going to need your help to take care of the house," he says instead.

"Yes," I say, as if in a trance. "Saturday is baking day, the smell of fresh bread and cinnamon; Sunday incense, get the kids ready for church; Monday lye, time to wash clothes; ammonia and bleach on Tuesday; can Wednesday; raspberry pies on Thursday; and Friday pluck chickens for the weekly tavern dinner. But what about the dandelions?"

Doctor Apfelbeck gives me a sidelong glance. "You're a strange man," he says before too long. "But she's lucky to have you." Grabbing his coat and hat, he heads for the door. "It's a shame your father's away. Meg could use him right now. What with your Uncle Robert in Milwaukee, Henry at university, and Eli off who knows where." He shakes his head. "There's a dire shortage of men in your household," he continues. "Your mother needs someone strong, Killian. And that will have to be you."

I want to say something. No one can take over for Mother, least of all me. There are so many things I don't know about her, things I need to know.

Alone in the fur room, I listen to the wind howling beneath the door, passing through the pile of furs in the corner, carrying their death smell to me. No one else smells them. The truth is, they've gotten so used to it they don't know the difference. They don't know that smells keep changing in death, the same way they do in life. Just after the animal's been skinned, the pelt smells sour, the smell of bile, but over time the smell softens to the bitterness of wood smoke. The scary part is that no matter how they smell in life, they all smell the same in death: bear, beaver, fox, or coyote, they all smell the same.

The wind keeps blowing, and it gets so I can hardly take the smell anymore. I get the wheelbarrow from the shed and pile all the pelts in it. The fox's fur is downy soft, the deer's hide rougher than my own hair. It should be the other way around, I think, or at least, since they all smell the same, there should be no difference in the feel.

Outside, the wind blows harder still, and the pelts fly from the wheelbarrow. I try to catch them, but all I can get are the bigger pelts. By the time I get to the river, all the smaller animals have flown, lynx, fox and rabbit escape on the wind.

I take the bear, deer, wolf, raccoon, and badger pelts that remain and throw them in the muddy pine needle water one by one. I watch as the pelts spread their limbs upon the surface.

When Father comes home and asks what happened to the furs, I tell him the smaller ones flew away, the rest chose water. He strikes me hard across my face, knocks me down on the front porch, the very same spot where I shuck corn with Mother. "Those pelts would have brought in enough to feed this family through the winter," Father says. He leaves me in the darkness of the cellar for a long time. But when I come out, he takes me in his arms and holds me so long it seems as if we've always been together like that. Then, he reaches into his pocket and hands me Mother's shiny, gold locket, the one she used to keep a picture of him in. Only now, it has a picture of Mother in it, her hair pulled back in a bun, her face irritated with sitting so long before the camera.

Father piles his gear on the front porch. When he goes inside to see Mother, I follow. She's sleeping and doesn't know he's there, and he doesn't wake her. He just takes her hand in his and kisses it, bringing each knuckle to his lips. Then he places his cheek on her fevered brow. He stays there awhile, breathing heavily. It's then that Mother calls out his name, as if she feels his presence in her dream, as if he's closer in spirit to her than he actually is. The sound of his own name startles him, and he backs away. I hide in the fur room, watching as he throws on his pack and heads down the road along the line of elms.

"Tell Frank, I'll be back soon." The wind carries his voice to me.

Mother wakes, coughing blood. I come running, bringing old towels, as I know she doesn't like to stain her fine handkerchiefs. She looks at me after I wipe away the blood. "Were you standing here before," she asks. "Or did I dream it?"

I don't tell her the truth. I don't know why.

All through her first bout with consumption, I take care of her, while Uncle Frank handles the rest. It's not bad. I take to her duties naturally. The doctor says her first bout is shorter than normal, and everyone thinks her speedy recovery is a sign she'll stay well.

Father comes back less and less often, aware of the rumors that death comes to our house on the backs of his pelts. And when he does return, his gaze is hollow, his movements slow, unsure, as if he's confused by the two men he's become—one who brings home money and food for his family, the other who brings home death.

Routine anchors me. Saturday baking, Sunday church, Monday wash . . . Mother, who is used to working harder than any beast of burden, watches, sometimes from her bed, other times from the porch steps. It seems to me that only her love keeps her sane, her faith in the continuity between mother and child. But then I catch her gazing out to the horizon, out beyond the elms, and I don't know. She loves me, yes, but that love is not all that keeps her alive.

At night, I read her the letters from Eli among the Hutterites. I read each letter over and over until a new one arrives, but Mother doesn't seem to mind. She makes sure to answer his letters right away, and when she can't write them herself, she makes me sit at her bedside and do it. Henry doesn't write, even though he's away at school. Mother says he's not gone so far as Eli. She says that of all a mother's children, the one farthest away has the strongest need to be close.

Sometimes she feels good enough to get around. On those days she goes right back to her routine, working alongside me. "I should have had you work with me all the time," she says. "We could have made enough raspberry pie to last 'til doomsday!"

When she's healthy, she works so hard it's as if she's never been sick. And she smiles all the while, as if she's keeping a secret that's in danger of bubbling out.

It's Friday, chickens and dandelions. We're sitting on the porch, sewing work clothes out of potato sacks. Even though Mother says she's having a good spell, I can see she's pale, and where her arms used to be thick they're chicken bone, her once-strong back curved with a weight I don't understand. I ask her why she looks as if she has the devil in her whenever she works.

"It's because I do have the devil inside," she says with a look as serious as any I've seen. "And work's the only thing that keeps him from getting out and raising Cain!" Then she laughs just the way I remember from the tavern, turning red in the face and gasping for air. I still don't understand, but I smile anyway because it seems so right.

The rest of the morning I try to stir up my courage to ask where the dandelion smell comes from. I'm not afraid of Mother; I want to understand. But I'm afraid the answer, like her humor, will be beyond me, and I'll have to settle for the feeling of rightness and not the thing itself. I know she doesn't help with Uncle Frank's wine. That's too simple. And besides, she'd say that's his business. She's got enough work to do.

Finally, as the morning sun rises in the sky, stirring the color to robin's eggs, Mother stands and holds the new trousers up against me. "Too short," she says. "You're a man now, I keep forgetting."

I think it's funny, though she didn't mean it to be. And, somehow, that gives me the courage to ask.

Mother looks at me as if she's forgotten that no matter how old children are they are always full of surprises. She takes me in her arms, and I inhale the scent of raspberries from the day before. It seems to me as if Mother is crying, though I can't see her face. But she doesn't want to let go, and I don't struggle as Henry or Eli might do. Sitting under the cottonwoods beside the river or wrapped in Mother's arms, it all seems the same to me. There is so much to feel, so much to let in, that it's impossible to distinguish one moment from another. I just sit and let it all wash over me. And now I feel the beating of her heart, the coarseness of her hair—like mine—and the stiffness of her dress, not yet warmed to softness by the sun. And as soon as the smells and the images they carry with them arrive, they're gone, overwhelmed by something else. If I don't let each moment go, I'm sure I'll drown in the next.

When I can no longer remember who I am, Mother releases me. "The greatest mysteries have the simplest answers," she says.

Jake Mulenbach stands in his overalls in front of the elms, his thinning hair combed over to the side just the way he used to, though now there's scant left to comb. In his right hand, which he presses to his heart, he holds a bouquet of dandelions.

Mother gestures him onto the porch for coffee, and he steps hesitantly, assessing me and my knowledge of the world. But Mother makes the decision for both of them, embracing him, trapping his arms and the dandelions between them, the yellow pollen staining Mother's apron and Jake's overalls. I want to ask if he comes every Friday. I'm afraid of the answer, but this time it's not because I don't think I'll understand. It's the opposite.

Most of the time, though, Mother doesn't leave her room, sometimes for so long the sheets smell like bile, and I think death is coming. I sleep beside her at night, pressing cold towels to her head, holding her as she shakes, using my shirt to wipe the blood from her mouth. On those days, I don't go out. It doesn't matter. The sky changes in my mind. It's Mother's changes that frighten me, the oak color of her skin, fading to gray ash. The way her skull is creeping out of her face, as if death is looking for her not from without but from within. Still, her scent fixes me to her.

I don't understand when it happens, but one morning I wake no longer sure what's in bed with me. The frail form, its skin as tenuous as a dream. It's not my mother. It's not the woman who takes my hands, teaching them how to knead bread, or holds me on the porch after we've returned from gathering berries, each of us tasting a few and laughing as the juice runs down our chins. The pelts have come back, I think. Borne by wind and water, they've come back to haunt me. They cover my mother now like a shroud, their bitter wood smoke smell keeping her from me. *Don't fly away with them, like Catherine!* I don't know if she can hear me. Perhaps if I wash her clean, we can start over.

TWO

SPIDERS AND SHADOWS
WALLACE | *Wisconsin*

Silky black and about a half an inch in diameter. It sits tucked behind the topmost log on the woodpile behind the house.

"Kill it," Father says. "Smash it with the log."

With the curiosity of a scientist or a criminologist, I tilt my head to peer beneath the spider, but I can't make out a thing. I take a twig and knock it to the ground. Before it rights itself, I spy the red hourglass.

"Step on it," Father says. "Believe me, it won't think twice about biting you."

The spider stills itself, as if it hopes to become invisible by not moving. I stare at it for a long moment. When I look close, I see the eight eyes staring back at me.

We don't read Plato's *Republic* in school. My father brought it home from the library, and we read it together each night. He explains the parts I don't understand. My favorite part is the cave, the fact that we are all prisoners doomed to watch the shadows play on the wall and think it's reality.

It dawns on me then that if I'm the prisoner and the spider the shadow, what does the spider see when it looks at me? Am I shadow and substance both? If so, then what determines me? I take the lemonade glass Mother set out for us and drink it down in one gulp, then carefully pull back the log and set the glass over the spider.

"What in the hell are you doing?" Father says, but it's only force of habit. He knows how my mind works.

I scrape the glass along the ground, until the spider is at the edge, its feet tucked up making a protective ball. I slide a leaf under the glass and in one quick action tilt it up. I carry it deep into the woods and let it loose. It wastes no time making for the cool shade of scrub oak. A jay perches on the lowest branch of an oak, watching us.

On the way back I wonder if spiders have directional sense like birds or other animals. If they can find their way home. I picture the hand of my father or mother, or even my own, reaching into the woodpile one evening getting fuel for the stove. I see the spider waiting in the darkness, watching. And I wonder what I might do if I encountered it there again. Plato says that justice is the result of a well-ordered soul. I say it is by our actions that we order it.

HOW TO OPEN A NAPKIN
WALLACE | *Colorado*

By the time I arrived in Seven Falls, the "Meg" was churning out more silver than the next three Colorado mines combined. Seven Falls was a respectable town of three hundred and fifty people, almost a quarter of them women—and not all of them hookers. J.D. Demings was feeling the competition from two other hotels and people didn't even bother to count the number of saloons. There was so much demand for goods that in '77 Pete Myers found the perfect excuse to retire as sheriff. Years before, the job had become too much for Pete. They needed a real sheriff, and that's where I came in.

I met Henry over a poker game at Guller's Saloon. He liked me the moment I quoted from Thompson's *Psychology of Criminals* as I gathered up my bluffed winnings. Rather than begrudging me, he offered to buy me a drink and proceeded to question me on my theories of the criminal mind. I told him my ideas about how crime was a disease like the flu or pneumonia. I told him that disease rose up wherever man felt a void, whether that void was spiritual, emotional, or physical, and that what he had here in his town was a lot of people walking around as empty as a Nevada well. He offered me the sheriff's job on the spot.

He insisted that a jail be built, though I told him that I would consider myself a first-rate sheriff if I never had to use it. And for the first couple of years, I did consider myself first rate. People came from nearby towns and as far away as Denver to see the empty cells. One night, someone even hammered a sign above the jailhouse that read: "Rooms for rent." I liked the sign so much I left it hanging there until the day I quit.

I wondered why Henry needed a jail when he seemed reasonable in so many other ways. But then again, I didn't come to my understanding of Henry and Elizabeth right away. In my line of work, it's the meticulous observation that pays off, the continual study of a person's daily habits. You'd be surprised to know that people repeat ninety-nine percent of their actions day in and day out. We are, to use a common figure of speech, "creatures of habit." It's the moment when we break the habit that the unconscious gives us away. And the habits of Henry and Elizabeth were not hard to follow.

Each morning at eight sharp Henry left Elizabeth in bed and made the walk to the mine to check on his affairs, though he knew Will Markey managed things perfectly well without him. At noon, he took lunch at Demings' Hotel, passing the afternoon in one of the hotel's suites, which he permanently rented as an office. There, he poured over topographical maps, searching for the location of his next mine. At six, Henry took dinner with a different member of the town's council.

Though Elizabeth scarcely rose from bed during the day, her patterns weren't any more difficult to figure out. Henry's brother, Killian, took charge of the household chores, even changing little Molly's diapers. Of Elizabeth's other exploits, I will not recount here. We all have our secrets. A lady is no different from a man in that regard. It's strange, but I believe sometimes, when I wake in the middle of the night, that it's those secret selves that later give us our strength.

And I noted how once a week, to keep up appearances, Henry and Elizabeth dressed up for a dinner engagement with various members of the town's growing upper class. So, one night, several months after I'd arrived in Seven Falls, when Henry had asked his wife to accompany him to meet the new sheriff, I wasn't surprised when Elizabeth walked into Demings' lobby dressed in a flowing green, taffeta gown, one that had clearly cost Henry a fortune. Nor was I surprised by the care in which she'd painted on her face or the light manner in which she held Henry's arm. What did strike me was the fact that while Henry entered the hotel covered with snow, his wife remained strangely dry, as if the softly falling flakes outside would rather dissolve into the air, disappear forever, than land on such a creature.

"It's my hat," she said, affecting a smile. "It protects me from the elements."

I laughed, as of course the wide brim of her hat was dusted with snow.

"My wife, Elizabeth," Henry pronounced.

"Remind me to get one of those," I said, stooping to kiss her offered hand.

"A wife or a hat," she replied pulling her hand away a split second too soon, a gesture hinting at nervousness, the need to hide.

It wasn't until long after we sat down to dinner that Henry broke the silence. "You better slow down, Elizabeth," he said. "Or they'll have to bring you another trout."

"Yes," I continued, eager to follow any trail. "Your healthy appetite suggests an active mind."

"It certainly couldn't be an active body," Henry said. "I mean, Elizabeth has little to do during the day."

Elizabeth finished chewing before setting down her knife and fork, one on each side of her plate. "How would you know what I do?" she asked, her jaw pulled tight until I was sure it would break. "You spend so little time at home, I mean."

Henry cut himself a large chunk of steak, but left it on his fork. "Observing behavior is Wallace's job, my dear," he continued. "So it's best to be on your guard. That is, if you have any secrets." He took the napkin from his lap, dabbed at his mouth and laid it between them.

Elizabeth dropped her hands to her own napkin in her lap. Held it there.

"Wallace swears he can stop a crime before it occurs, before a man even thinks of committing it." Henry shielded his face with his glass, inhaled the wine's aroma.

Elizabeth's gaze flitted about the room, as if she might take flight at any moment. She's like a bird, I thought. A fearful bird.

"It's my firm belief that no man wishes to commit a crime," I said in hopes of stilling her. "No one wishes to do evil." It worked. Her gazed fixed on some pattern on the wallpaper.

"Tell Elizabeth about the book you're writing," Henry said before finishing off his glass of wine.

"When a man commits a crime, it's only because society has failed to hear his calls for help. The crime is his final cry. It's the same whether it's a crime against society or a crime against the self." I stopped and sipped my wine.

Slowly, almost imperceptibly at first, she turned her head toward me. "And what, then, does your trained eye see in me," she said, speaking just slightly above a whisper.

She folded the napkin in her lap into smaller and smaller squares.

"What was it Keats said," I asked, not really sure where I was going, but trusting in it just the same. Any lawman learns to rely on intuition early in his career. "Beauty is truth, truth beauty, that is all ye know on earth, and all ye need to know."

"Yes, I believe that's it," Henry replied. "I like that."

"I do, too," I said. "Except, I think Keats had it wrong."

"A poetry critic as well," Henry replied, feigning surprise.

Elizabeth's face betrayed nothing.

"It makes for a pleasant poetic illusion, but there's no truth in such simple equations," I said, feeling on more solid ground. "If anything, beauty acts like a gossamer curtain, or like green eyes," I ventured, pausing. "For a brief moment it gives us a glimpse into what lies beyond, but just as quickly, it distorts that glimpse, its shimmering surface refracting the light until we are no longer sure of what we see at all."

"I didn't know your knowledge included literature and philosophy," Henry said. "You are an accomplished man."

Elizabeth placed the napkin she'd been folding in her lap on the table. "If you know so much," she said, her voice taut, "what are you doing in a little mountain town lost from civilization?"

I smiled. She had heard everything. "The difference between knowing and doing," I replied, "is greater than the space between stars. Greater even than the vast distance between one person and another. I believe that's the truest thing I've learned yet in this life."

As if in answer, one of the folds in her napkin sprang open.

THE CITY OF MY SOUL
ELI | *Colorado*

I had not expected the town to be so big. People stirred everywhere, kicking up the dust from the dry spring road. I walked through that dust as if into a new life. And there standing before me in the middle of town was Henry. He'd had word of my approach and waited in his best suit, now brown with the road dust, a smile stretched across his face like he'd known all along I'd be coming, as if he expected it was the only thing I could do.

We embraced, and the people stopped milling about and whispered of the stranger who'd arrived and walked into the mayor's arms. He wanted to know what I'd been up to these many years, but how could I find words to tell him? How do you describe the transit of the soul?

He told me of his accomplishments, the mine, the burgeoning town, and the latest schoolteacher, who'd actually agreed to stay on for another year. And I told him of my journey across the Great Plains, of my time with the Hutterites.

"Eli, you've made me very happy," Henry said as we walked toward his home along the river. "The town will finally have a preacher." He put his arm around me then. "And I will have both my brothers."

I stopped and stared straight eyed at my brother. "I'd heard you took Killian with you when you left, but I didn't believe it," I said, wondering if Henry was still the same boy I used to go fishing with, the one who would make me put the worms on his hooks.

"He's our brother," Henry replied, his arm firm about me. "Mother would have wanted us all together."

"He killed our Mother," I said, stepping out of his grasp. "He threw her in the river when she lay sick, when she still had breath in her body and hope of recovery." I spat upon the ground before my brother.

"They don't know what happened," Henry replied. "Uncle Frank told me himself. No one knows."

"Killian does."

"How can you say that?"

"They found her body on the bank near Stratford."

"They questioned Killian. He didn't know anything."

"The Lord knows what happened," I said. "And he will judge Killian for it one day."

Henry looked askance at me, perhaps wondering if he'd made the right decision to invite me to his town. "Our house wouldn't get on without Killian," he said. "He runs it the way Mother ran the house when we were young."

"You have children, Henry, and a wife?" I asked, realizing only then how long we'd been apart, how many things had changed.

"Yes," he said, smiling once again. "Come, you'll meet them too." And with that he turned and walked toward home, assuming I would follow. I did, but not as closely as either of us would have liked.

Three of God's blessings, two boys and a girl, ran to greet us at the door.

"Children," Henry said, taking each one before me.

"This is your Uncle Eli." Killian hovered in the background, dressed in the same style of overalls he used to wear years ago, his hands in his pockets.

Silence settled upon us. The kids, having a true sense of when things are not what they seem, looked back and forth between Killian and myself. All except little Molly, who waddled over to Killian, only to be scooped up in his big hands. Henry stepped back, hoping we'd settle things in our own way.

"What are you doing hovering in the background," I said to Killian. "Come give your long lost brother a hug." I didn't know what made me say it. I told myself it was the Christian thing to do. Killian was my flesh and blood after all. Yet I sensed a deeper reason, one I couldn't admit.

Killian didn't move, and I wondered if, like the children, he
sensed things too. We stood there, waiting. No one saying anything.
I almost asked after Henry's wife, but then Molly bounced up and
down in Killian's arms impatiently, and he let her down.

I stepped toward him, hoping to reassure him or, perhaps, myself.
And then he came forward, slowly, giving me a big hug. At first I
stood stiff, but then I remembered Mother holding me that same
way, her long, broad arms like home. And it was as if I could see
her face before me. It was too much, and I laughed, making a joke
that Killian was getting bigger than a bear and stronger too. The
kids laughed at that, like they knew something I didn't. And for a
moment I thought they were all mocking me. I tried to push Killian
away, but he just kept on holding me. And the more he held tight,
the more I began to panic.

"Killian!" I shouted. "That's enough!" I pried one arm loose
and pushed and pulled, shaking him. That was when Henry forced
his hand between us. "Killian!" I shouted again. "Are you some
sort of devil?"

Henry looked at me then like he wished I wouldn't have said that.
He'd driven his body between us now. The two youngest, Webb and
Molly rushed to Killian, each grabbing a hand.

"I'm sorry, Eli," Killian said, his head low. "I'm sorry."

"Sorry for what?" I asked, though I knew he was talking about
what he'd done to Mother. I knew it even if he didn't.

"You've nothing to be sorry for, Killian," Henry said.

"We are all sorry," he said.

Henry and I sat in the salon as the children played around us, and
Killian occupied himself stirring the beef stew in the kitchen.

"So, where's this wife of yours, Henry?" I asked as he poured
himself a glass of wine.

"I don't suppose you drink, being a man of God and all,"
Henry said.

I paused before answering, wondering if Henry's diversion was intentional. "I'll have a glass, thank you."

We talked of his accomplishments in the town, and my brother was quite proud, but I couldn't help notice his attention turning toward the staircase every minute or so, and I wondered if he was as proud of his wife.

The upstairs floorboards creaked. For a moment, the children stopped their play and listened to the back and forth movement above. Then, just as the aroma from the stew wafted through the house, a light footstep sounded on the stairwell, clear but distinct. A pair of feet covered in bedroom slippers came first into our view. Then the woman, entirely dressed in a luxurious, silk bathrobe, but a bathrobe nonetheless. Her brown hair was unkempt and matted on one side, as if she'd just risen from sleep. She didn't appear to notice me until Henry said, "Elizabeth, dear, please say hello to my brother, Eli, who has come to us after living among the Hutterites."

Elizabeth stopped dead at the bottom of the stairs. "Why didn't you inform me earlier, Henry?" she asked, forcing a smile.

"I didn't want to disturb your sleep," Henry replied. "Besides, his arrival was unannounced." For a moment, there passed between the two of them a look not unlike hatred, though that would be too strong of a word. Rather, it was the earsplitting look that passes between two people when they both acknowledge that they are tired of all each has to offer.

Elizabeth immediately regained her composure and joined us in the salon as if nothing was out of the ordinary, taking a glass of wine, sitting opposite me on the sofa, and adjusting the folds of her robe. It was then my body burst into flame.

"I'm sure your brother is very tired, my dear," Elizabeth said. "Perhaps he'd like to lie down before dinner."

Sweat beaded my brow. I set aside my wine glass and slid my trembling hands beneath my legs.

"Eli is going to be our preacher," was all Henry said in answer. His words, too, burned me, and I wished he would take them back.

Elizabeth's face angled ever so slightly, unreadable. "Well," she said. "A preacher." She rolled the stem of her wineglass between her thumb and forefinger. I felt sure I would be consumed at that very moment. "I wouldn't have picked him as a preacher," she continued. And though her hands remained bare before me, it was as if I could sense her fingernails digging into her skin, as if she wanted to tear away the outer layer of herself, the same way I had mortified my own flesh for the impure thoughts that had sometimes crossed my mind. I lay awake all night that first night in the bed they'd made up for me in the guest room just below their own bedroom.

I lay awake thinking back to that moment in the salon, the moment Elizabeth and I were joined by hatred of our own flesh, and I knew that someday I would give in to that flesh, that someday I would have to see her if I didn't leave the town the next morning. I spent all night thinking of how I'd run from home after the horse, how I'd tried to escape the weight of my father and the burden of my sick mother's love. I thought of how I'd run from the Hutterites and kept on running across the plains.

And then I remembered the words of the Lord in Joshua eight: *For they will say, 'The Israelites are running away from us as they did before.' Then you will jump up from your ambush and take possession of the city, for the Lord your God will give it to you. Set the city on fire as your Lord has commanded. You have your orders.*

And I knew I could run no longer unless I too would be like the Israelites. Instead, I would keep myself from burning. I would take possession of the city of my soul.

WHAT LOVERS SHARE
HENRY | *Colorado*

I lie back upon the bed, cover my eyes so that I no longer have to see the dying light as it strips the heavy makeup from her face, as it sheds the purple boa from her neck. She kneels down before me, takes me in her mouth, this woman who is not my wife.

I lie and wait for the feeling that will tell me why, how a body can fall away from a home only to land in the bed of another.

"Henry, can I have a word with you?" Will Markey said, standing below the entrance to the "Meg."

"What worries you, Will?" I asked, pretending I didn't understand.

Will tucked his goose-bone pipe in his belt, something I'd never seen him do. I'd always assumed he went to bed with the thing in his mouth. "I'd rather we talk behind the stamp mill," he said, already walking in that direction.

It was a five-stamp unit, with beams three times as tall as a man, and it was going full bore, the cam lifting the stamps and letting gravity pull them to the earth. It was clear enough Will didn't want anyone to hear what he had to say. The dust billowing from the earth choked, and I covered my mouth with my handkerchief.

"It's not easy to confront someone," Will began the moment I rounded the machine. "It's the hardest thing in the world to admit when something's wrong." Forgetting it was not there, he reached for the pipe at his mouth. "I mean it's not in our nature to admit when we've been had, Henry. For a man proud as you, I mean." He rested his hand upon his pipe, as if fighting the urge to take it.

I waited, expecting him to say more. The drumming of the stamps shook straight to my marrow. It seemed to work at him, too, as he finally pulled the pipe from his belt and filled it with tobacco from the pouch in his back pocket.

"What are you getting at, Will?" I wanted to make him lay it out for me, not because I'd imagined he'd been one of them but because he'd known and not said a thing for so long. He was my foreman after all.

"The men are digging where they shouldn't be, Henry," Will Markey said after a time. "They're stealing what's yours." Then he lit his pipe and puffed until the smoke between us was good and thick.

"Why do you think that is?" I asked, honestly wanting an answer. The stamps grew louder until it seemed my body shook with them.

"I reckon when a man loses respect for another man, he'll do just about anything," Will said. "And if that other man doesn't respect himself, he'll take just about anything."

This was not the answer I expected.

Will puffed awhile longer, then turned and walked down toward the sluice.

"Does that include you?" I shouted out on impulse. Will Markey turned, looked at me askance, assaying what kind of man he worked for. He shouted back an answer, but I couldn't make it out. I didn't ask him again.

That afternoon, I walked to the top of La Nana, looked out over the town of Seven Falls and beyond to where the river joined with the Blue heading north through the fertile valley. For a moment, I thought about following that river, about starting over without the worry of a town.

At dusk, I came down and stood at the entrance of the "Meg," saying good night to the men as they left the mine for the night. Something I hadn't done in a long time.

I entered my home only to find Elizabeth rising mothlike from beneath her sheets and into the night. She sat at her dresser combing her hair while I stood staring at her, wondering at her nightly metamorphosis. Still, I could not bring myself to speak, to give voice to the body's knowledge. It was only when she turned away from me, when I saw how the slow curve of her neck had changed, how the smooth lines of her back now looked like deep striations, that I forgot myself enough to speak.

"I would like you to stop," I said, my voice barely above a whisper.

Her arms fell to her side. She sat upon the bed, and I waited, aware that if I was not careful, I would become the moth and fly to her.

"I'm not sure I can," she said after a long moment. And that was all she said.

"Can't you see who you are?" I asked. "When you look at yourself don't you see all that we've made together?" But I doubted myself even as I asked it. I had not known I would be capable of ignoring so many things, of enduring the lack of respect from my men and my wife, until now.

"I've never had that sort of clarity of vision," she said. "I don't know who I am until I act, and even then it's all so murky."

"That part I understand," I said. "Your actions have made my vision cloudy as well."

The faintest hint of a smile fell across her lips.

"I ask you again. Will you please stop, for both of our sakes?"

She said nothing, but poured herself a glass of water from the nightstand. I needed so badly to go to her, to hold her in my arms and forgive her everything, but instead I said, "For God's sake, then, please be discrete."

The light is gone, and her face with it. I close my eyes for I do not want to see as this woman rises and spits my fluid into the bedpan sitting on the wash table.

"I'm thirsty," I tell her.

She washes her face. With her mascara and lipstick gone, this woman smiles grotesquely and tells me she has just the thing.

"Whiskey," she says, sitting beside me on the bed. Her dank smell repels, yet I let her take my head in her hand, lay it upon her upper arm and feed me the drink. "It quenches your thirst no matter how parched you think you are." She takes a sip after me, and we both lie there in silence.

Normally, I wouldn't drink from a glass that has touched the lips of another, particularly someone of her calling. I allow her to give me sip after sip.

But no matter how much I drink, my throat remains dry. And I know Elizabeth and I share that much.

THE SCENT OF DESPAIR
ELI | *Colorado*

It was most difficult at night, for at night I could scent the pith of her floating down from the room above. I covered my head with the pillow, recited the Lord's Prayer, then Psalm 23:4: *Yea though I walk through the valley of death, I will fear no evil: for Thou art with me; Thy rod and Thy staff comfort me.* I tore my sheet and pressed the strips into the cracks in the floorboards above, sealing the space under the door with my coat and still the smell suffocated me.

I was preaching now, giving my sermons from the schoolhouse until the church was built. The people of Seven Falls entrusted me with their souls, and I would not disappoint them. I talked of temptation, how we are, all of us, tempted by the devil, and they believed because they felt the tremor in my own voice. I talked of how we are put upon this earth to help one another, but that sometimes, though we fight against it, we will do our brothers harm. And they nodded their heads because they, too, had felt this duality in themselves, the desire to do good, the need to do evil.

And each night I lay awake fighting both the scent from above and the beast inside me. Sometimes, to distract myself from my torment, I would play the game of guessing at the nature of her smell. Cinnamon, no. Honey, no. Not sweet. The smell of an autumn sunset. Closer. But each time, just as I thought I could describe it, wrap words around it, the scent faded, and I was left only with what it did to me.

Other days, when I preached at the mine, I felt sure she could not breach the heavy dank odor of earth, the sulphuric aroma of blasting powder, of burros and men who had not washed for weeks. And as I lie there, attempting to quiet my mind, she seeped into my skin like an underground stream, saturating my pores. She carried me down further until I traversed the dark damp of the deepest shafts.

Nearly a year passed before the answer was revealed to me in Job 28. I will find my way, I said, and I marched to the schoolhouse that Sunday ready to deliver a sermon the people of Seven Falls would talk about for years after.

There are mines for silver
and places where gold is refined

The trembling of my own voice, its weakness, startled me. But that same quivering took hold of the people. Even the men in the back, squeezed into the desks meant for the children, leaned ever so slightly toward me.

Iron is won from the earth
and copper smelted from the ore.
Men master the darkness.
To the farthest recesses they seek
ore in gloom and deep darkness.

The men and women all nodded, as if they knew of what I spoke, as if they could see into the darkness of my own heart, when they could not even see into their own.

Man sets his hand to the granite rock
and lays bare the roots of the mountains;
he cuts galleries in the rocks,
and gems of every kind meet his eye;
and brings the hidden riches of the earth to light.

And now I held them in the palm of my hand. It is the moment when any man of God knows to deliver the breath of the Holy Spirit. "Ye who search the darkness beware!" I shouted, and then

finished the scripture:
> *But where can wisdom be found,*
> *and where is the source of*
> *understanding?*
> *No one knows the way to it . . .*

How could I not have been prepared for the last line?

The Lord holds all cards and refuses to let even his servants know what hand he will play. I wavered upon the pulpit, sweat dripping from my brow. And the people waited. I stuttered then started again: "God alone understands the way to it." But I could not finish. Her scent held me even here, the smell of vertigo and obscurity.

"Come on, preacher, give us the Word," Frank Foote shouted, and the crowd grunted its assent.

It is the smell of dead grass, the smell of falling cinders, of emptiness and absence. It is the smell of the forsaken, and it was upon me. I opened my mouth to speak but no longer knew what I said.

> *And he said to mankind:*
> *"The fear of the Lord is wisdom,*
> *and to turn from evil,*
> *that is understanding."*

And what does the Lord say to one who is lost in the darkness?

I woke, startled by the fact that the scent had penetrated my dreams. The smell of insanity, of the horrible indifference of stars. Yes, for a moment I was sure that was it. Then, like a dream, the image faded, and I knew I was no closer. I must leave or die. So, I began to pack my things, but the dark splash was upon me, its legs encircling, squeezing me until I could no longer breathe. I followed her, downward, ever downward until she was waiting for me in the shadows of the kitchen, waiting without knowing what she was waiting for. I tracked her scent through the dark until the force of her stillness stopped me. I waited until she could scent me too, not understanding that we'd recognized each other long ago. Each of us breathed in slowly, deeply, until we were buried in the other, until we coughed up air, needing still more space.

Before I knew it, I was upon her, but she did not stop me. I tore at her silk robe, the one she wore that first night. I ripped it open, searching for the answer I thought I'd found in scripture, looking for the way God promised. And still, she did not respond. What had I expected? Arms about me, lips pressing against mine, hands pulling me closer or at least beating me away? She did none of these things. Instead, she turned away from me slowly and bent herself over the kitchen table, offering her darkest regions to me.

I fell to my knees as if in prayer, burying myself in her, losing myself completely now in the darkness. No moan escaped from her mouth, no cry of pleasure or anguish. Nothing. In fear, I tried to climb back to the surface, fighting the thick odor of my own craven desire, but it had gone too far. On my feet again, I plunged into her, sure that she could not stand the weight of my need. And still she did not move. I wanted to cry out, to scream to her to stop: *Do not smother me with your silence! Do not take me with you into that chasm of darkness!* But all I did was shudder over and over as I spent myself inside her.

Only after, as I lay slumped upon her back, did she turn, her eyes two black pits in the darkness. And she clasped my head in her hands, her fingers fated reigns upon my face. I searched deep within her gaze, looking for some semblance of myself but found only barren trees rising from those orbs. "Elizabeth, . . ." I wanted to say more. Words alone could transform our carnal act. But no words came.

I collapsed behind the teacher's desk that served as my pulpit. They rushed to me, fearing that my passion for the Lord had been my undoing, not understanding the terrible manner in which He works.

"He feels the words of the Lord too much," they said. "He is too good a man!" They dragged me outside, sat me in a chair in front of the schoolhouse.

"Leave me be!" I shouted, waving the crowd away, but they would not move.

As I shut my eyes, I could feel them closing in about me. "The preacher has taken on too much," one woman said. "He needs his own church," said another. "No one can preach in a schoolhouse, especially one that used to be a saloon." And then the words that bit me like a snake even as I tried to shut out the world. "Who else but the preacher will show us the way?"

I never went back to her house. Instead, I took a shack up near the mine, and still I cannot escape.

FINDING THE LOWLY
Killian | *Colorado*

I tell them, wake, it's right under your skin. Webb and Molly don't understand and look at the skin on their arms. Henry Jr. says he doesn't want Molly coming along, he says babies just slow us down, but I tell him it's Molly that we're going to follow.

"Not again," Henry Jr. says to me, pulling on his pants, his eyes still glued shut with sleep. "Why can't we go on a real adventure instead of following the little ones?"

"How do you know if you're on an adventure until you're on it?" I ask him in return, but he just shakes his head, too tired to respond.

I dress Molly while Webb pulls his clothes from the dresser, throwing them all over the floor until he finds his favorite shirt and pants. Then, to keep her warm until the chill air of the autumn morning breathes itself away, I set Molly inside my coat, the same way I used to set Webb, and she squeals with delight, liking it there more than Webb ever did.

Henry Jr. heads straight for the kitchen cupboard, hoping to scrounge up some food, but I tell him that's part of the adventure. His eyes finally open. "Raspberries aren't going to fill me up," he grumbles. "I need some real food."

"All you have to do is look," I say.

"I know, it's right there under my feet," he replies, finally giving up or at least realizing the cupboards are empty.

We walk right out the back door and along the path until it takes us above the river. The smell of raspberries drifts up from the gulley below.

"I can't see where they are," Webb shouts. "I can't see the river any more."

"I know," I reply and close my eyes. I have been here for years, I think. Maybe I was never anywhere else.

The children know by now to still their bodies, to quiet their mouths and listen. The crunch of the dried and yellow aspen leaves beneath our shoes nourishes us; the steam rising through the cracks in the ground quenches our thirst. Molly squeals from inside my coat and points at me. "Lian," she says, as if I'm all there is in the world.

Then I realize she's not pointing at me but at the white stains that cover the remaining cottonwood leaves. "Woodpecker," I tell her and Webb looks too, though Henry Jr. says he already knows this and keeps walking.

"It's called finding the lowly," I say.

And, as if in response, Webb stops and lowers his hand to the ground. A spider with a body half the size of a silver dollar crawls onto his palm. It's striped yellow and black like a bee.

"Can't eat that," Henry Jr. says.

"No, but you can feel the tickle of its legs upon your skin," I say. "A spider can walk on water, can you do that?"

"Only Jesus can walk on water," Henry Jr. replies, taking a stone and throwing it down into the gully.

"Jesus and spiders," I say, and Webb laughs before setting the spider back on the ground.

I take Molly from my coat and set her on the ground, she's off running immediately, and it's all we can do to keep up. Then she stops.

"Uncle Eli always brings his gun," Henry Jr. says, stopping a short distance from Molly. "He says nature allows us to measure who we are."

I nod along, though the heavy, root smell from the aspen grove before us draws me forward. I can't shake the smell of gashed earth, the crushed grass and tumbled places where she rolled on her back, scratching an itch. The smaller marks, the scuffs everywhere in the dirt, signs of play.

"Lian!" Molly screams. The trees shake before her.

"There's something in there," Henry Jr. says. He and Webb stay where they are.

I know it's not the trees that excite Molly. She smells it, too. She has my nose, a dog's nose.

The trees tremble and shower Molly with gold rain. Webb jumps up and down, shaking his hands like they're wet, and he needs to dry them.

Come back, Molly. But I'm not sure if I've said it or only thought it because at that moment the bear dam emerges from the grove followed by her three cubs. She's big, the biggest I've seen, and she's swaggering around, trying to make herself look even bigger.

As if from the force of its breath, Molly falls back on her butt. She stays there. She looks so small, and the bear is too big.

Without thinking, I put myself between her and the bear. One of the cubs runs toward us, thinking I mean to play, but the mother swats it back with one large paw, and the cub goes tumbling into the brush behind her. The dam wags her head from side to side.

"Is she a mean bear?" Webb whispers from behind me.

I signal Webb to be quiet. But then the dam raises her nose to the air, scenting us, and I wake to the bits of raspberry sticking to the sides of her gaping mouth. I feel the fetid stench of her breath upon me, the thick weight of hide. The flaring nostrils engulf me. I smell my own blood, my shit, and the fungus that eats away at the skin on my elbows. My tongue lolls about in my mouth, fighting off that wretched odor. I'm roaming in circles, looking out through narrow eyes, drizzly eyes. The icy waters call, steam rising from my skin, the sharp berry smell demanding me. I want to run and go on running, to eat deer scat, to claw myself upon a tree. And again I wake.

I shout, clap my hands as much to fight back the dream as to scare the bear.

The dam lowers her head, wet eyes gazing into me. She shakes her head back and forth violently and growls. A warning. The air quivers, but I am rooted to the earth. The dam waits, completing the ritual. I clap again, loudly.

Suddenly she turns away, nudging her cubs with her nose, grunting after them. The cubs run in a line up the mountain, and the mother lumbers after.

"Lowly," Molly says, shaking her own head from side to side. And I smile because I know she's right. We can't find the lowly. But I'm not sure if she means that we can't because we are the lowest of creatures, or if she is saying that everything is so big, everything including us. I want to ask her, but she's already running back to the others.

SPINNING
Eli | *Colorado*

I liked the scared girls most, the ones who, no matter how many nights they've been in the dancehall, bow their heads and slouch their shoulders before they approach. It was the tension, the uncertainty as they wavered between the intoxication of seduction and their own sobering abasement that made them interesting.

I hadn't come for the dancing or for the women, not for the music either. I came each night to drown the memory of her in sweat and beer, to purify myself with whiskey. And each night, I took in the rank air, replaced her scent with the musk of bodies grinding close, the harsh tang of pine floorboards encrusted with silver and dirt.

I didn't watch them directly but rather through the mirror that backed the bar. Cluskey's wife, Ellen, had imported the mirror from France. It took ten men to lift the monstrous oak frame, and the exertion probably ruined Old Cluskey's back. He could never lift anything more than a bag of sugar after that.

The girls all wore white pinafore dresses and would dance with you for twenty-five cents. And for five cents extra they'd even dance a mazurka. Business had been good of late, maybe because the mine was still down after the accident in the second shaft and the miners finally had a chance to spend some of their money. So each night the girls danced, picking miners from the bar whenever they found themselves empty handed or their purses light.

They knew not to pick me. And it wasn't because I was the preacher. I hadn't preached a sermon in two months and told them I didn't think I ever would again.

One of the scared girls liked to twirl. I watched her on the nights when not even the whiskey helped. When she danced with a man, she threw herself into spins. She'd spin and spin until the man got tired of waiting, until the scared look transformed itself into a glassy-eyed smile. Then she'd thank the man for dancing with her and pull another one off the bar so she could get to spinning before that smile faded. *If you have hips, if you have hips, trim your dress in the parasol style* . . . The music played on.

I never danced with her, but each night when I'd had enough, when my clothes stunk with the smells of the dancehall and I could safely go back to the shanty by the mine I now called home, I would walk up beside her. I timed my walks to coincide with her spins, and each time, as I left the dancehall, my hand found hers and pressed a silver dollar in it. She never stopped spinning, but she'd taken note.

At night, as I lie upon my straw mattress, a voice glides in upon the wind, seeps between the undaubed cracks of my shanty. *If you have hips, if you have hips, trim your dress in the parasol style* . . . It calls me. There are many ways to make yourself empty, and one of them is spinning.

I rise and kneel at my bed, beseech the Lord to save me. Tonight I leave You. I renounce all that You demand of me. In town, Frank's fiddle calls to me, a woman's voice sings: *Go to sleep, go to sleep, go to sleep in your baby's arms* . . . . And I follow the voice, letting it fill my mind, my soul, until You are gone. *Go to sleep, go to sleep, go to sleep in your baby's arms.* The smells of Cluskey's dancehall waft upon the wind as I walk down Main. But I don't need them anymore. The voice will carry me. Your scent no longer haunts me. No longer. Your name no longer demands. I name you myself. Elizabeth. No longer.

At the bar, I drink whiskey after whiskey, watching her spin. And still the voice continues, *Balance yourself, balance yourself, balance yourself in your baby's arms* . . . And though I know that she is not the one singing, I could swear that the voice comes from her, thrown out upon the air as she spins faster and faster.

The singing stops. The spinning girl twirls to a halt. Her reflection approaches me in the mirror. Her hot breath falls upon my neck, and I hold tightly to my whiskey. Her hand rests upon my shoulder, light as silence. The delicate trace of her finger cascading my arm. She presses her lips to my ear and whispers one word, but that one word calls me out of myself, so that I now see us both standing before the great mirror. "Spin," she whispers, nothing more. Then she clasps her hand in mine, and I'm gone.

She knows that if you turn the horse's head the body will follow. It's easy to guide an animal when you understand its nature. Dance with me, her hand says. Spin with me, her hips whisper. And I watch myself go out on the floor with her.

The music kicks up again, and we begin to spin. *Go to sleep, go to sleep, go to sleep in your baby's arms* . . . The dancehall is falling, and still I'm spinning. The world is falling around me, and I'm spinning, spinning. And though she does not speak, her own name echoes in my mind, growing louder with each revolution: *Charlotte, Charlotte, Charlotte!*

THE POWER OF NAMES
ELIZABETH | *Colorado*

When you least expect it, it begins to snow. It falls all day and into the night, and still I have not moved. I pull the blankets tight about me, fearful that I am not ready, that I will never be ready. But then there is a knocking at the door. I roll over, pull the covers over my head. Henry's out, I know this. The children are asleep. Why doesn't Killian answer? The knocking comes again, harder than before. And then a voice I recognize, though I have tried to forget it.

"Elizabeth," the voice says. "You are the only one I trust."

I open the door, take his arm and lead him inside, then place both his hands within my robe. It is not enough. His hands are ice, and he withdraws them.

"Charlotte's in labor," he says. "And we can't get word to the midwife in Montezuma because of the storm."

I pull my robe tight about me and turn toward the kitchen.

"She's not doing well, Elizabeth," he goes on. "She's in too much pain."

"Why me?" I ask, as if there could be an answer.

He offers none.

"Give me a minute to dress," I say. And without thinking, I go to my armoire and search through the evening dresses and ball gowns, the bustles and corsets until I find the plain housedress Henry'd bought me in hopes it would lead me to housework. Then I lace up my Balmorals, as they seem the most likely to weather the snow. Before I go down, I stand in front of the mirror. Without a hat, my head feels lighter, almost dizzy.

"Henry keeps the snowshoes in the shed," I tell Eli. "Get them while I gather some supplies."

Flickers of firelight from inside a handful of cabins beckon through the falling snow. We do not stop to partake of the warmth

hinted at there, though I wish we could. The half-mile hike up La
Nana is too much. The cold and wetness have seeped through my
Balmorals, and my feet are beginning to ache, as are my lungs.

Just when I think I cannot take another step, Eli cuts through a
large growth of scrub oak to the left, then behind the massive, snow-
covered boulder that hides his cabin from the world. He opens the
door, and I'm surprised that it is not death I smell, but the sweet
basil smell of a house well cared for, and a trace of persimmon that
hints of love. I did not know Eli had found such happiness.

The one-room cabin is bathed in the rich yellow light of an oil
lamp, with the firelight occasionally deepening the air to orange.
Charlotte lies on the bed at the far end of the cabin, tight-lipped,
sweating far more than she should be.

"Breathe, my darling," I tell her. "You are wound too tight." I'm
surprised at how easily the words come, how quickly I slip into
another role. She looks at me like she doesn't know how to open.
So I take her hand in mine, and with the other, I caress her head,
leading her to the place I know so well.

We sit like this for hours, until I see that life has found a way into
her space, and she wants to tighten again. "There's nothing you can
do about this tightening, my dear," I tell her. "It is our lot in life.
But it will be over soon."

The nod of her head is the only sign that she is conscious at
all. Her body contracts. She screams, pushing because she has no
choice. The cycle repeats itself again and again. And with each cry,
with each push, I feel the snow falling layer upon layer, as if I have
no choice either.

The baby's head crowns, downed with blonde hair. I see the eyes
scrunched tight, the face pickled, yet determined, and then I see
the pulsing blue cord wrapped around the neck.

"Hold off!" I shout, and Charlotte looks at me as if I've just
asked her to do the impossible. Still, she does it.

I work my fingers between the neck and the cord. I'd always

thought I had delicate hands, slender fingers, but they seem like brute instruments at the moment, utterly incapable of fine movement. The cord is tight about the neck, the womb always exerting the pressure to leave it. Still, I work my fingers in and gently pull the cord over the head. It is wrapped not once but twice.

And then the baby's out. I wrap her in a towel and with a warm cloth begin to clean her.

"A girl!" Eli whispers.

I'd forgotten he was there and realize only now that he'd been there, watching everything. I'm glad he's happy for a girl. It will help, I think.

Charlotte screams so loud I'm startled. Her eyes roll back into her head. "It's all right," I tell her. "It's only the afterbirth." But her cry hints at something more than that, and I fear I will not be up for the task. My own first birth echoes in my mind, and I find myself repeating the words of Jess Carter.

"Fetch moss! Lots of it!" I shout to Eli, and, without hesitation, he's out the door.

I swaddle the baby and lie her upon the ground at my feet. She watches me with eyes far too intense for one so young.

"I want to push!" Charlotte shouts, and then it's clear to me.

"Yes, push!" I tell her. "You're having another." She responds, drawing strength from recesses that only exist for me as dim patches of memory.

"This one seems in a bigger hurry to get out," I tell Charlotte, as the baby pops out without event. When Eli returns both girls are swaddled and suckling at their mother's breasts.

"You missed half the fun," I say to Eli's stunned face. But he no longer hears me. He is at his wife's side, caressing her and cooing at the babies. I can hardly believe it is the Eli I'd come to know during the heady passion of our nighttime encounters. I stay for the afterbirth, and, with Charlotte's consent, I carefully wrap it in my shawl to take home to store. Later, after the snow melts and the ground thaws, I will bury it beneath their front door to bless all who enter their house, to remind them of the life that made its brave entrance in the world here, the double life. And as I gather the soiled sheets for cleaning, I hear Eli ask about the names.

"Alice and Jane," Charlotte replies, touching each of her babies on the forehead.

"They are nice names," I say, "beautiful names," and then I leave them to their newfound family. Walking home through the snow, carrying the essence of that new life bound up in my shawl, I realize it is time to give myself a new name, a name to go along with my new profession.

And so, in the morning, when I walk in the front door of our house and Henry greets me with a frantic, Elizabeth, where on God's earth have you been, I reply casually: "Elizabeth died on the mountain last night, buried beneath the snow. From now on you can call me Nell."

Henry's mouth opens wider than Charlotte's nether region, something the old Elizabeth would have thought but never said. Nell not only thinks it, she says it with such a guffaw that Henry steps back, unconsciously reaching for the accustomed handkerchief in his breast pocket, though he carries none in his silk pajamas.

DANDELION WINE
KILLIAN | *Colorado*

I look out from the shed where I wash the dandelion blossoms and watch the rain fall light as stardust.

"Uncle Frank used to say that after two glasses of his wine a man could remember how to fly," I tell Webb, who sits at my feet handing me clumps of the yellow flowers. "He used to say that the same way we are born knowing how to swim and then forget only as we get older, we are born knowing how to fly."

"How do we forget?" Webb asks, Molly settling into his lap as if she has all the time in the world to hear the answer.

"The question is why," I tell them, but they just keep staring blank-eyed as if they didn't hear me, or didn't want to. "And the answer to both is that I don't know, except to say that our minds aren't big enough to hold all the things we need when we grow up and to still remember how to fly."

"Tell us how to fly, Uncle Killian," they say in unison, and Webb hands me the last of the dandelions.

"I used to sit at my Uncle Frank's knee the same way you're doing now," I say, the memories resurfacing as if they'd been there all along. "And he'd tell me the same story I'm about to tell you, only his story was about how he remembered how to fly and mine is about how I remember because it's something I have to remember each and every day."

I hand the children a bag of oranges and lemons and give them each a knife to cut away the peels. Just four years old, Molly handles the knife as if she was born to it. Like Eli skinning a deer.

"Did you grow wings like an angel?" Molly asks, and I tell her we don't need wings; all we need to do is stand so still that the air around us becomes invisible.

"But air's already invisible!" Webb tells me, and I laugh as I squeeze some of the lemon and orange juice into the pot.

"Before you make it invisible, you've got to make it visible," I say. "Close your eyes and stand still until you feel the air thickening around you, tickling your skin, then open your eyes." Both children stop peeling, close their eyes, wait a moment, and then open them, staring into the space before them.

"I don't see anything," Webb says. Molly's eyes glow with excitement, and I wonder what she sees.

"That's because you're already on your way to forgetting how to fly," I tell Webb. "We're making this wine none too late!"

Webb and Molly hand me their peels, and I throw them in with the dandelions, then add a few cloves and a little ginger for good measure.

"Tell us!" the children scream once again, and I look into their eyes, searching the memory for a more solid surface on which to ride.

"I'm standing under the elm all night," I tell them. "It's cold but the wine I drank keeps me warm, and Uncle Frank tells me that cold makes the air even better for flying, so I wait while my breath surrounds me."

"Why is the cold better?" Molly asks, but Webb shushes her, putting his hand over her mouth, which she then bites. "Why?" she repeats.

"All things are more alive in the cold—even the air," I say with a grin.

"Just say what happens," Webb says, covering Molly's mouth again.

"I stand there until my weight falls away like boulders from my body," I say. "I keep my eyes closed until I'm sure the air is shimmering, and when I open them I wait. And then the wind picks up, throwing me through the branches of the elm and into the sky."

"How does it feel to fly?" Molly asks, the fire in her eyes stronger than ever. And it's then I know that she won't need the wine at all.

"It feels like falling," I say, sitting upon the ground with them.

"Does your stomach tickle?" Webb says, thinking of the times I would toss him in the air.

"Your whole body tickles," I say and both children giggle as if I'm tickling them at that moment. "The tickles enter through your feet and hands, through every pore of your body."

"I don't know if I'd like that," Webb says.

"I don't either, and that's what makes me think about the fact that I'm flying, and soon I'm dropping to the roof of my house," I tell them and their eyes open wide.

"What do you do?" Webb asks, and Molly's so still, wrapped in Webb's lap.

"I untie the lines of my veins," I tell them. "I drop the ballast of my bones and soar upward past the startled birds."

"How far do you go?" Webb asks, throwing the last of the orange and lemon peels in the pot. And I'm sure he's thinking the more he puts in the higher he'll fly.

"I rise and burn past stars," I say. "I fall and slip past moons. The pulse of the universe pushes me until I'm sure that I'll fly forever, maybe never return home."

"How do you get back?" Webb asks. "What about your mother? Does she look for you?"

"The rooster crows, and I return right back to the same spot where I stand under the elm."

"Did your mother ever find out?" Webb asks.

"No," I say. And that keeps them silent for awhile, wondering why I never told my mother of such a miraculous event. "Some things we have to save as secrets for ourselves," I whisper. "If we want to keep the magic alive."

They nod their heads in unison.

"Now, the rain has stopped," I say. "So, who will help me carry this pot to the fire pit?"

Webb is already grabbing the pot handle with both hands, but Molly is slow to rise. She might already be flying.

I get the fire going, and we sit quietly around the boiling froth until the smell alone can lift you from the ground. I add yeast and tell the children that it must sit over night and that tomorrow we'll bottle it, but then it must stand for another month for it to have its full effect.

"A whole month!" they scream together, then break off into their separate complaints.

"That's forever," Webb says.

"I don't need wine," Molly tells her brother. "Besides, Father says kids shouldn't drink wine anyway."

"This wine is special," I tell them. "It's worth the wait."

Webb marks each day with the question of when the wine will be ready. For the first week, Molly joins him, but soon she moves on to other things. It seems that her sure knowledge in her own abilities dulls her interest, that part of the thrill is wondering whether or not we can do something.

But then one morning a week before the wine is ready, Webb tells me that he remembers how to fly.

"Uncle Killian, it's so simple, and it's not like you said at all!" he nearly shouts at me. "I don't stand still. I run as fast as I can, and as long as I keep my legs moving, I can fly."

"Don't you get tired?" I ask.

"Not for a very long time," Webb answers. "I think this kind of running is not so difficult as the other."

"Will you show me?" I ask him, and he beams in reply.

"Follow me behind the town. Where they're putting the new railroad in," Webb barely has time to say it all before he's off and I'm following.

The newly laid track makes for a long running area, as they've cleared the trees for ten yards on each side, and it runs straight along the spine of the town.

"Just watch, Uncle Killian," Webb says. "And don't blink because before you know it I'll be higher than the clouds."

"Okay," I want to answer, but I can't get a word out because he's off and running. At first, I think he's running pretty fast, but he's just kicking up dirt, that's all. And then I see the soles of his shoes glistening in the sunlight and it looks like they're missing the earth entirely, and I remember the bees, the way the sunlight reflected off their backs, and I think yes, he's found the secret. I almost miss him as he flies past trees, soars over the town and out past the trinity of mountains that guard the western sky. And then he's gone.

Dreams pull us from this earth. Molly knows this and now Webb knows it, too.

RESURRECTION
WALLACE | *Colorado*

For years, each winter they'd set up camp near the Blue and watch from a distance the goings on in town, as if it was their only diversion. Hundreds of them, dressed in buckskin, mink, and jackrabbit, the chiefs among them wearing a mishmash of European clothes, the more formal the better. They always kept their distance, so the townsfolk and the miners didn't get nervous. Sure, there was the occasional incident, but, all in all, we got on pretty well, each group sticking to its own world. At least until Meeker. After that, it wasn't only the townsfolk who got jittery. The Indians did too. The year of the massacre, when winter was over, they packed up and left, following the Blue downstream. I thought that was all I'd ever see of them. Heard the cavalry came and rounded them up, took them to Utah where they could live on reservation land, if you call that living.

But then six months ago, on my way back from Kokomo, where they needed an extra sheriff to help quell a miners' revolt, I spotted one of them carrying water from the river. She was bent with the weight of it, carrying the water in her arms as if it were a child. Her thick, black hair matted to her shoulders. Her wide, flat face so cracked you'd think you could fall right in. If I didn't know better, I would have sworn she was some sort of animal, a porcupine, the way she walked bent over like that, sort of waddling.

I got down from my horse and hid low in the scrub oak for fear she'd take note. But she must have been too preoccupied with her work, as she didn't appear to see me. It was only much later, as I sat at my desk in town recalling the image, that I realized I'd never been so close to an Indian before—no more than twenty or thirty feet lay between us.

I followed her, leading my horse through the brush to a clearing where her family had set up camp. Her husband, at least I assume it was her husband, sat alone off to the side of the camp, his back to me. A girl of not more than eleven or twelve emerged from their brush wickiup and took the water from the woman. As she returned to their shelter, I caught a glimpse of yet another girl within, perhaps a couple years older than the first. But it was the woman who kept me rooted in place, the way she never stopped moving, as if each action were choreographed, just another step in a dance she'd performed countless times. I knew it was dangerous to remain. The man would soon sense my presence. Yet, I could not help but watch the woman quietly tilling the small garden they relied on for nourishment. As she worked the hoe, she sang with a voice only for herself, and I wanted to hear that voice, to know if the words matched the steady rhythm, the quiet assurance of the woman's actions.

I didn't fool myself into thinking I could keep the cavalry from them. If they returned for another roundup, I could do nothing. Yet, I felt that somehow in my observance, in my acknowledgment of their existence, I would be doing them a great service. And secretly, I knew that if I could but understand a word of the woman's song, she would be returning the favor of my visit many times over. And so I returned, often.

And then summer came, and I found it more and more difficult to get away. Henry's silver was drying up, and the miners that risked everything to get here, coming now from all over the United States, did not react well to the dearth of opportunities. Some just moved on, but many stayed, looking for ways to cause trouble rather than make an honest living. I hired deputies, but it was still all I could do to keep even the semblance of peace.

"Wallace," Henry said, "It's time for you to wear the gun that goes with this office," he said. He'd marched over because the night before had been a particularly bad one. Two stabbings and three armed robberies. I reminded him of what I'd told him upon our first meeting. An oath means nothing if you break it when times get tough.

That very day one of the miners who couldn't find work, a man who said he'd come from just about every town east of Seven Falls, started spreading rumors about Utes that avoided the round up, Utes that were preying off of homesteaders and storing their money in holes dug deep beneath their wickiups. I didn't like the look of him, not at all. The man couldn't keep his mouth shut. And what made it difficult to silence him was the fact that he spread silver along the bar as if the veins of the "Meg" were still shining bright and running miles into the earth.

"Where'd you come across that kind of money?" I once made the mistake of asking inside Percy Hart's saloon. I should have known better than to get him talking in front of a crowd.

"From the hides of the heathen Utes," he said, grinning, bearing a silver tooth. I've taken it upon myself to finish the job the cavalry left undone."

The men around the bar burst in, shouting over each other. *Where'd you find them? How'd you whip them all by yourself? Can we come with you the next time?* It was all I could do to break the men up at that point. The damage had been done, and I'd helped to make it so.

That night I went to warn the Ute family, to make them leave. I didn't care that they couldn't understand me, that the woman's husband might even try to kill me, thinking I meant them harm. I had to drive them further down the river. It was then I noted the tracks, two riders who took the long way around so that their trail would seem to be coming from the opposite direction of town. I doubled my pace.

About a hundred yards before reaching the camp, I came across the body of the woman's husband, knife in hand, two bullet holes in his chest. I was right, he would have killed me had he seen me that day or if I'd tried to warn him on this one. The second was that of the older girl, also holding a knife, a knife they used to make her slit her own throat. She must have come at her father's first cry, running to aid him, instead of running away as he would have wished. The third body was that of the woman. She was stripped naked, beaten about the face, blood and dirt shoved deep into the cracks and lines that marked her age. Why the men chose her for their pleasure, I do not know. There are things about the criminal mind that no book will ever reveal. I covered the woman with the torn remnant of her own dress, a European style affair she must have traded for. I bent my ear to her mouth, no longer hoping to hear her voice, but to catch a hint of her breath.

Nothing but my own frantic breathing. Was there not another? How many bodies had I counted?

A stifled scream from inside the wickiup. I grabbed a melon-sized rock, jagged on one edge, and ran to her. The drifter lay atop the girl, his pants around his ankles, thrusting himself inside her. I recognized the man cheering and laughing beside them as Ben York, a miner who'd arrived the year before and never caused any trouble. Without thinking, I raised the rock above my head and brought it down hard upon the drifter's skull. He made a dull gasp in surprise, then let out a low moan like a sigh. I brought the rock down upon his head again and again until the skull gave way, softly.

"Wallace, have you gone crazy?" Ben screamed. I rose and turned to him. And something in my face must have scared him, because he ran without waiting for an answer. I started after him, thinking to kill him too, but the girl's moan stopped me. I dropped the rock and pulled the drifter from her body. Her eyes were shut tight, blood splattered about her face.

My only thought was to wash her face, her body. She raised no arm against me, made no attempt to stop me, not even when, kneeling upon the bank of the Blue, I lowered her in its icy waters. Her eyes opened with a shock then, and she looked about as if waking from a deep sleep. I took off my own shirt, and scrubbed every part of her, then sat holding her in the morning sun.

I couldn't return her to her camp. I couldn't give her that last memory of her family. But where could I go? Back to town was impossible. I was an outlaw now.

As I wrapped the girl in the blanket I kept tied to my saddle, she said one word, the only word she would ever say to me: "Nahoonkara." I didn't understand the word, could only guess at its meaning. Yet it sang to me as I imagined the old woman's voice might have done.

Ever since Nell had become a midwife she rose before the sun came up and sat upon the bank of the north branch of the Seven Falls that ran behind her house and watched the first blush of light as it warmed the river. I'd noted everything in the town but especially those things that had to do with Nell. I'd often watched her sitting upon the damp earth, leaning back against a pine, her pant legs rolled up so that her calves could take in the sun. She'd sold her fancy dresses, her hats. Always, she tilted her head back against the trunk, her eyes closed as if she could see better that way. And though I knew it was wrong to watch her so, I found I could not turn away. After a time, I matched the rise and fall of my breathing with her own. Only then, would I allow myself to leave and go about my business.

Nell received us as if the reason for her morning ritual had always been to prepare for this one day. And once again I felt the peace of inhabiting the same space with her, of breathing her air. Without a word, she took the girl from my arms and set her down upon a bed of moss and pine needles, then went inside for her things, returning a moment later with boots and a simple dress that looked to fit the young girl. She never asked what had happened, how I'd come to care for this dark child. It was as if she understood that lives were made up of moments like these. All else was watching, waiting.

"The dress was mine when I was her age," she said, her lips parting ever so slightly. "It's the only thing I had left from before my parents died."

I nodded and took the clothes from her.

"She will have to start over, too," Nell said, almost as if talking to herself. Then, when we finished dressing her, she grabbed both the girl's hands and looked her over. "I'm going to save you the trouble I went through," she said. "Your new name will be Dee." The girl stared back at her, but Nell didn't try to explain herself further. She just took the girl's hands, placed them upon her chest and repeated the name. "Dee."

And those were the last words she spoke that morning, preferring the depth of our silence. I set the girl upon my saddle and grabbed the reins to mount my horse, hesitating only a moment. It was then Nell's hand brushed my shoulder. I did not turn for fear that if I did I would never leave. And my time was through in that town. It did not matter. I understood the message the touch conveyed, the warmth that said we know who we are, the soft grace that said we know what we have become for each other. And I held tight to the promise of that touch.

I followed the Blue as it wound its way north, after a week of travel coming upon a family of homesteaders who agreed to take the girl so long as I also left them my horse. They seemed good enough. Christian folk. And they promised to raise her well. So I walked away from her as I walked away from Nell, as I walked away from the town of Seven Falls and my life as a sheriff.

As I walk even now, my soul heavy with starlings.

THREE

THE LONG SNOW
Narrator | Colorado

The morning of November seventeenth, 1886, the snow began to fall on the town of Seven Falls and didn't stop for three months. In the first days of the snow, the trees waved gently back and forth, as if trying to catch the snowflakes. But soon the trunks stiffened under the cold, the branches sagged beneath the weight, until finally, after a week, even the pines gave up and set themselves to endure what would be the longest snowfall in their memory.

Coyotes yipped throughout the night of the seventeenth and eighteenth, calling their kind together, as if their very survival depended upon the strength of the group. Bears dug in deeper than usual and prepared for a very long sleep. And the deer and smaller animals, the raccoons and porcupines, squirrels and badgers, all ran about frantically, knowing those first few days might be their last.

The snow fell slowly day after day, in no hurry to blanket the world. And as the snow fell, and the trees grew still, and the animals grew quiet, time itself slowed. Life slowed. So that by the fifth day if you stopped to listen all you would hear, if you were very quiet, was a low creaking deep inside the wood.

After two weeks, any building in Seven Falls less than two stories was completely buried. It was as if the miners' cabins and the general store, the meat market and the post office, the bank and the smithy all ceased to exist. During this time, people still thought they could wait out the snow, and they generally stayed in their homes or shops. The town became a graveyard, the two-story buildings forming multiple headstones that peeked out from the white surface: Guller's and Percy Hart's Saloons, Carl's Dancehall, the twin bell towers of the church on one end of town and the schoolhouse on the other, and the entire second floor of Demings' Hotel rising above the arctic expanse. The guests, not understanding that they would be trapped there for the next three months, made the most of it, taking their drinks out on the balcony where they sat and watched the snow fall, as if they'd just arrived from the tropics and had never seen this crystalline miracle. And in truth they hadn't, for the snow continued to fall week after week without cessation. In those first couple of weeks before some of the guests began to panic, they sat on that balcony staring out at the world like birds from the treetops. And even those who panicked never forgot the gift of their new perspective, the way in which they in turn were watched by a great horned owl from a neighboring tree, a family of downy woodpeckers from the grove a few yards off from the balcony, and countless mountain chickadees who stared back from their upside down perches along nearly every tree and even the sides of the hotel itself. The way in which it no longer mattered who lived where or which saloon had the nicer front as everything was buried in white.

One particular guest, an architect named Isaac Hamlin, saw, in the pattern of indentations that marked the criss-crossing of the side streets with Main and the mounds that represented each building along them, a vision that would haunt him for most of the rest of his life, until he eventually moved to San Francisco, where he designed a cathedral, the chapels, cloisters, and naves of which traced the same ghostly pattern he'd seen during what he proudly told other San Franciscans was the greatest snow in the history of the known world.

After a month, even the two story buildings were buried, and people understood that this was no normal winter storm, that their lives might be irrevocably altered. The guests in Demings' Hotel descended to the main floor lobby and huddled there, praying for help.

And, as Christmas approached, the first people emerged from their homes and shops—not slowly or lethargically like bears from their caves, but rather, like ants digging their tunnels beneath the ground, for they had to dig their way from one building to another. Their lives depended on it. The first tunnel went from Cluskey's Dancehall to the hotel, as Carl had heard the cries for help and knew that Demings couldn't possibly have stored enough food for all, and that the guests, being mostly city folk, would be unaccustomed to tightening their belts.

The second tunnel went from the hotel to the general store, and they didn't have to dig very far, for thinking along the same lines as Carl Cluskey, Pete Myers had already dug over half way to meet them. The celebration that ensued was only one of many during those first couple of weeks of the second month of the snow, for as one tunneler came upon another it was as if two brothers who had been estranged for years had finally met. Even the most bitter of enemies were seen to hug each other, tears running down their cheeks, swearing an end to whatever conflict had been between them, if they remembered the conflict at all. It was that way with Martin Watson and Frank Foote, who after hugging each other over and over and sitting down beside their shovels to laugh about the reason why they'd not spoken in the last year, could not even remember it had been because Frank had refused to pay Martin for the re-shoeing he'd done on Martin's horse. Frank was not a cheap man. It was just that he'd felt Martin had simply hammered the same shoes back on again.

Soon the townsfolk were walking the dark tunnels of early morning to feed the animals in their barns. Then, they ventured out on other mundane tasks, most of which centered around how to keep the fires in their cabins lit: poling a hole to the surface for the stove pipe, clearing ash, carrying wood or coal from the storehouse. And their routines remained largely the same, albeit beneath the surface of the world. The supply trains had done an admirable job of keeping the tracks clear and were still able to make it with supplies until nearly the end of the second month. So, for the people of Seven Falls, the long snow didn't mean that life had to stop, but rather it took on a different form. Women met for tea, taking turns in one another's houses and occasionally gathering within a hollowed out town square that had taken shape as several tunnels converged. The women actually enjoyed snuffing out their candles one by one, then sitting, sipping their tea under the eerie blue glow of the scant sun sifting through the layers of ice and snow.

The blue glow was the only way the townsfolk could tell the difference between night and day. They'd gotten used to carrying candles and lanterns as they traveled in the tunnels, no matter what the time. Though, somewhere near the end of the second month, Lulu Giberson took to walking about without a candle even at night. She said it put her in touch with her other senses, with the deepest part of herself. And soon the other women followed. Clubs formed, as it became the thing to do. They found it even more intoxicating to stumble upon each other in the darkness, as they moved about, their hands before them, tracing patterns along the icy walls of the tunnels. The women said the men grew jealous; they didn't like the idea of their women meeting in the darkness like that. And so, the men formed their own clubs and took to walking about without the aid of lights as well. In fact, it quickly became the favorite pastime of the town, particularly as people made their way to and from Cluskey's Dancehall throughout the night. And Carl Cluskey was happy to keep the dances going, Frank Foote playing his fiddle well past the witching hour. No one knows how many romantic liaisons were formed or broken during those few short weeks of total darkness, but many such unions did occur, and they were not all between lawfully married men and women.

Something about the anonymity of the darkness liberated the townsfolk, so that when they looked back on that time, they often smiled, though a few tried to erase it from their minds altogether, preferring to forget not only the anonymous other, but also the secret person they'd discovered within themselves deep beneath the snow. For it was not only encounters out of wedlock that occurred, but occasionally women with women and men with men.

Though no one talked about the subterranean trysts in public, conversations did sometimes occur in private;, but even on those occasions people usually made excuses for their behavior, saying they couldn't tell who was who in the dark. When others heard such excuses, they recognized them for what they were: attempts to rationalize what cannot be rationalized, to explain away that animal part of ourselves that resists explanation. For all the tunnelers understood that one didn't need eyesight to know who was who, because their other senses had grown quite acute. That was partly wherein the pleasure lie. Each tunneler attuned himself to the crunching snow beneath his boots, and every tunneler's sound was unique. Lulu Giberson's "Below-the-knees" squeaked as the high heels scraped against the frozen ground, while Pete Myers' copper-toed "Wolverines," as he liked to call them, had a sort of machine sound as they punched the earth. Of course, the sense of touch was the most heightened of all.

As one tunneler heard the approach of another, the anticipation of that touch was almost too much. Searching fingers found each other, then moved over hands to wrists, feeling downy hairs or coarse skin. And eventually, hands made their way to faces, the contours of which took on a completely different aspect under the sight of touch. But the explosion of the senses that occurred beneath fingertips was nothing to what happened once lips met flesh.

The encounters didn't always follow that path. Sometimes, the emotions stirred, the sensations felt were almost too much for the tunnelers;, or, perhaps, they were just what was needed, and they would simply stop and hold hands, listen to the stillness about them, feel the weight of it. They would sit or stand there like that until the sound of Frank Foote's fiddle called to them through the snow.

At what point in the night Frank actually took up his fiddle no one was really sure, as time had begun to lose all meaning for the tunnelers. All they knew was that sometime after their world turned completely black, the music of the fiddle would call to them, at first softly through the snow; but as Frank picked up steam, it was as if his music carried some of the heat generated by his fiddle and used it to melt a path through the snow, calling louder and louder. And as they entered the third month of the long snow, the trysts between private couples gave way to large gatherings of folk in the town square. The town would gather together in the darkness shortly before Frank began playing, as if the anticipation of the sound now joined them completely. They didn't talk or socialize during this time. In fact, if asked a question they would not even have answered. It was as if the town had undergone yet another metamorphosis, and they were one creature, standing together, absorbing the silence, and soaking in the faint blue light, the result of the full moon that signaled the beginning of the third month of snow. They stood beside each other, often holding hands, taking in this new alchemy until the fiddle called to them. Then, as if they were one mind, they would move together to the dancehall, no longer able to distinguish the unique sounds of each boot upon the ground, for in this final phase of the snow all boots sounded the same.

Once inside, they broke up into couples and danced polkas and mazurkas, but all in the dancehall knew that though they were pairing off, though things seemed to be going back to the way they had been, things were not like that at all. They understood that a community had formed, one deeper and surer than any they had known before, one that would be needed if they were to withstand the events that would unfold in the month that followed, the events that began as they emerged out of necessity from their subterranean world to walk once again upon the surface.

THE LARVAL DREAMS OF CHILDREN
NARRATOR | *Colorado*

Sometime during the end of the third month of the long snow people stopped going out again. It was as if they'd swallowed the snow, and now it had stuck inside them, thick against the walls of their stomach, piling its way up their throats until they could no longer breathe. The secret meetings and nightly dances stopped, though occasionally someone swore to themselves as they sat in their houses that they heard the faint whisper of Frank Foote's fiddle.

Food grew scarce, but the townsfolk sat as if frozen to their chairs, the call of hunger stifled by the weight of winter. Word was the supply train that came from Denver had gotten snowed in. The railroad had fought valiantly to keep the track open, but the thirty-foot drifts finally overwhelmed the C&S Boreas, and it sat out the final month of snow somewhere in the Ten Mile Canyon, the snowed in passengers on the train surviving only by eating the food meant for the residents of Seven Falls and other towns. But food alone wouldn't have brought the citizens of Seven Falls out of their icy sepulchers. They wouldn't have smelled it even if they'd had the desire to eat, for their sense of smell along with all desire had been smothered, the air pressed to such a density it's a wonder they could breathe at all.

The town of Seven Falls would have died that month. And later, when the last of the snow melted at the end of May, it would have revealed a perfectly preserved town with people curled up in their beds or rocking in their chairs, blankets thrown over them. It would have been that way, a town-sized tomb, if it hadn't been for the children, for it was the children who led the people out of the darkness of their homes and back into life.

During that last month of the long snow, the children too grew languid, as if their blood was thickening and icicles were forming in their veins. It was then the miraculous change occurred, as so often happens with children. They throw off their old skins, the selves that are no longer of use or that have grown stiff and boring with age, and they emerge ready to play. And so, the children tunneled out, making their way up through the schoolhouse bell tower, carrying snowshoes, sleds, and homemade skis, anything that would help them adapt to their new life on the surface.

Once there, they looked for areas where the drifts hadn't piled quite so high, areas that would make for good sledding. And they mounted their sleds and skis and slid from the top of the schoolhouse bell tower down to the rooftop of Guller's Saloon, then hiked up to the top of Demings' Hotel and down again to Pete Myers' General Store. But the children didn't think in these terms. To them, the buildings had disappeared, existed as faint webs in the recesses of their memory, and they'd already swatted those webs away. All they saw were a series of hills and valleys stretched out in white, calling to them, demanding that they play until, exhausted, they climbed back down the bell tower and into their beds only to begin again the next day. It didn't matter that they were hungry. Hunger had also been forgotten.

Carl Cluskey was the first to follow. Though he'd told his wife, Ellen, if their three children were going to play that hard they were going to need food to eat and supplies were all but gone, what really woke him from his stupor were the giggles floating gently down like bubbles through the layers of white. So he took his snowshoes and rifle and ascended the bell tower. While Carl was emerging into the new world, Eli made a similar decision in the mining camp up the mountain. The miners had actually been better off as their camp was protected in large part by La Nana herself and so only received about half the snow, which was still enough to bury their small cabins.

The men with children emerged first, either inspired by their children's adaptability or driven by the knowledge that they needed to feed them. Martin Watson and Galway Giberson soon followed and joined Carl on his first hunting expedition, but Eli remained to himself, disappearing for days at a time up the valley between La Nana and her sister. Both Eli above and Carl's group below left unsure if they'd find anything, and at first they didn't, for they hunted in the old style, looking for life on the surface. Each adapted in their own way.

After three days of returning home exhausted and empty handed, Martin Watson finally suggested to Carl Cluskey that they try digging by the river to see what might turn up. They uncovered a family of frozen deer, the meat perfectly preserved. Soon, instead of hunting expeditions where the men were equipped with rifles, they went out in groups of three, equipped with shovels, hoping to emulate that first successful expedition. And they did, quickly realizing that if they followed the river, they were bound to come upon more animals dying for lack of water in the frozen desert.

Higher up the mountain, Eli still hunted by the old method, his only adaptation aiming his sights to the trees instead of the ground. Each day, Eli returned with birds slung about his neck: owls and hawks, woodpeckers and jays. At first his daughters, Alice and Jane, refused to eat, for they loved the birds, but Charlotte, their mother, soon learned to cook and prepare the meat out of the girls' sight, and then they ate willingly and ravenously. Eli enjoyed watching them eat; in fact, he found he was happier than he'd ever been. Often, during those days, he'd sit in his chair by the fire, watching how happy his girls were after they'd filled their stomachs, and, perhaps for the first time in his life, he felt he had a purpose. For this reason, each time he left for another day of hunting, he found himself torn by the desire to simply sit and watch his girls and the happy responsibility of needing to provide for them. And it was at just one of these moments, when Eli stood in the doorway wishing both to stay and to go, that the long snow finally stopped. It did not slow down before stopping completely, but rather, after three months of snowfall without abatement, it ceased in an instant, as if the sky had gone empty and couldn't possibly expel another flake.

Sunlight broke through the clouds almost immediately, not content to wait another moment after having waited so long. Eli stepped forth, blind in the new world. It took him several minutes before he could see again and many hours more before he could truly welcome the punishing glare. And immediately, he went out into the woods, for he knew now was the hunting time, that for this day alone the world and all the animals in it were half awake. The animals would stumble upon him in their search for food, and he would gather all he needed in a few days and then return to spend the spring with his family.

He did not understand that the day after a heavy snow is the most dangerous day of all, particularly when the harsh sun works so hard to warm the earth. In the cold, the snow sticks stubbornly frozen to the surface of the mountain, but as the mountain heats up, great slabs of snow slough off and slide away, slowly at first, but as the friction generates more heat, the slabs slide faster, crushing everything in their path before finally coming to rest.

THE SPEECH OF TREES
KILLIAN | *Colorado*

I wake and find myself in the snow far from town.

I walk over the frozen world, and with each flake that falls upon my skin my heart slows. I don't mind this slowing of blood, this thickening of life. Soon my body will match the body of the world.

I walk, and the air fills with the tinkling of bells. I don't know if it's the snow or if Uncle Frank is dressed as Santa again or maybe it's the little bells they've taken to hanging on the children so they can find them if they venture to the surface and get lost or buried in the drifts.

I walk, and the higher I climb the more I hear. The trees are the loudest of all. From deep inside their sap-stilled bodies, they cry out under the weight of all that snow. The world is pressed to their pace. They speak to me in creaks and groans, telling me what eternity really means.

THE WARM BREATH
Eli | *Colorado*

Sorrow falls quickly here, in the mountains. Cuts us from our families. Cuts us from ourselves. Cuts us until we bleed white.

Before the snow silenced my life, morning came, the last leaden clouds scraping the sky, forcing out the darkness. And I gazed into the sun, not yet able to see. Like Saul, I was blinded by the light of heaven, and, like him, I trusted in God to guide me as he did when he sent his servant, Ananias. How can we know our trust in God is well-founded when he tests us so? How could I know, my darling Charlotte, Alice, and Jane, that he would sever me from my body?

That afternoon, after my sight returned, I shot two rabbits and a crow. I should not have killed the black bird.

Vengeance falls quickly here. Dusk came, and I spied no other creatures. I would have better luck the next day, I told myself, as I packed the snow beneath my feet and built my shelter of ice. After skinning and cooking the rabbit, I sat within my shelter, the dim glow of the dying embers casting shadows upon the wall.

When morning returned, I gathered my voice, my eyes, the life remaining to me, and tied the last rabbit to my belt. The crow I left buried inside the shelter, but still it followed me, pecking at the back of my neck as I turned toward home. I would not stay out another day.

Pines broke the surface, first one, and then another. They'd not been there the day before, or at least I'd not been aware of their existence. Now they demanded to be seen. The world was changing before my eyes, and I asked myself, who was I to see it?

Cruelty falls quickly here. And I'm plagued with the memory of that beauty turned to heartbreak and horror.

It was then I saw the buck, ribs pushing at skin, legs wobbly with the exertion of staying upright, of balancing atop the fragile crust. He nibbled at the exposed bark as I brought my rifle to my shoulder and sighted him. The blast echoed through the valley but by the time it returned to me, it carried with it another sound, a deep rumbling and shaking as if the earth were sloughing off her skin. The buck fell, spilling its life into the snow, but my gaze turned to La Nana not so far away, yet far enough that all I could do was watch as the top third of the mountain gave way, one giant slab of snow and ice, falling, sliding downward, driving all the snow before it until it became its own mountain of tumbling snow. I called out to Charlotte, told her to run, to gather the children, but my voice was buried in the growing roar. Only later did it return, and then I scarcely knew it.

Justice falls quickly here. There is a long white scar on La Nana, and I follow that scar down to my heart. The only tree left standing marks where my house once was, and that is where I dig.

All morning, I tunnel down, piling mounds of snow on each side. I hear the cries of others up from town as they search for friends, loved ones. *Double Tom, are you here? Big Jim! Will, Will Markey, tell us if you live! Wilbert Marshall, you never turned down a bottle of whiskey before, so come out and get some now!* I dig until I find the splinters of my house. Henry and Nell stand by me then, but I pay them no notice, not even when Nell screams and falls writhing upon the snow. My girls lie sleeping in the remains of their bed, sharing their long slumber, Alice's blonde hair entwined with Jane's brown. I find Charlotte nearby on the floor. And now there is nowhere to run.

Henry and Nell tried to take the bodies down the mountain, but I waved my rifle in their direction, and they understood.

Long I slept beside my family, waking sometime in the darkness, sometime in the light. It made no difference. Then, as if in a dream, I took my hatchet to the lone tree, cut out its heart. With my long knife I spent the night carving my heart. I needed to shape my anger and my grief, put them somewhere where they could sing.

And all the while I carved my fiddle, I could feel him there watching me in the distance. I shouted to my brother, but still he stood, so faint I could barely make him out in the woods beyond.

"You're a devil!" I shouted to him. "Like Father, you bring nothing but death."

He did not answer, just stood there as he'd done before with the roan. As he'd always done.

"What dark pact have you made that you roam the earth so freely?"

Again, he did not answer.

I rose then, turned to face him directly. "Come here, Killian!" I shouted. "Come here and taste the warm breath of the Holy Spirit!"

And still he did not come.

I laid my grief like a skin over the fiddle, and waited. When morning came, I played a sweet song and prayed for someone to wake me. It was then He made himself known, told me my mission had just begun, my life had only now begun.

The townsfolk returned shortly after first light, better equipped with shovels, ready this time to carry the frozen bodies to town. "Listen closely," I told them as I stepped from the pit where my house once stood. I left my fiddle alongside my wife and carried with me my rifle instead. They did not take heed to my words, so I fired into the air, and they were more attentive.

"Listen closely to the words of the Lord," I said, as they gathered about me. "As told in the second book of Esdras . . . "

They stood rapt.

But it is for you, Ezra, to tear out your hair and to let every calamity loose on those who have disobeyed my law. My people are beyond correction.

And still they stood. So, I told them what the Lord asked me to speak.

VOICES

KILLIAN | *Colorado*

Spring has done its work. Near the banks, the snow is only a few feet deep, the ice upon the surface only a foot or so. And even then, the river finds a way, patches of dark clear water push to the surface, needing to breathe. Sinkholes in the snow strengthen the river's voice, murmurs bubbling up, reverberating off the ice.

I kneel upon the bank to better hear, the wet soaking through my overalls. I place my ear upon the snow and listen to the voices rising from the deep.

Remember me ....

What am I doing lying about well past dawn? There's work to do. With Eli gone, there's double the work, and the girls will be hungry soon. I'll wake them with potato pancakes. I think there's even a little syrup left. Jane loves extra syrup. And look at this mess! The girls will clean it up before they get any pancakes. I don't know. It seems the more I clean the dirtier things get. How did this snow find its way inside? Eli, I'm going to need your strong back before the day is over. Just look at me, how soft I've become, complaining about a little snow. Grandmother always said she had no time for words when there was work to be done. Alice? Jane? Where are you, my dears? There's going to be pancakes!

Bees flying into my skull, the voices continue.

Remember me. . .Where's my pipe, my tobacco? No sense going on if I can't have my tobacco. I'm a man of few needs. All I ask is for my hat, my goose-bone pipe, and a dry place to lay me down, and now I don't have a damn one. Life doesn't amount to a whole hell of a lot if a man can't have a smoke when he wants to. Ah, there you are, my beauty, let me dust the snow off you, let me warm you in my hands. The sweet smell of fudge still lingers from the last smoke, clinging to the air like a whisper. Now as soon as I find my tobacco, I'm getting the hell out of here. Damn the "Meg", Henry. It's no good anymore anyway. La Nana has had the final word. All there's left for us to do is to walk away and start again.

Watch where you swing that shovel, Percy, you almost took my head off. Martin, you got any tobacco? All I need's a pinch.

Carl don't sit there like that, staring into the snow like you can't see anymore. This is nothing. You've got three beautiful girls. So get up off your butt and tend to them. Stand up and be a man! All I need's a little damn tobacco . . .

And the buzzing voices only grow louder.

Remember . . . The snow piled us, sinners one atop the other. A tomb of ice and snow. I will shape the snow about me until I have four walls to keep the Lord with me, a new church to call the souls to heaven. But the voices are unbearable. I will build the church God wants, but first I must drown the voices. I know Lucy will give me a drink. Just one little drink to stop the voices. She knows I'm good for it. She knows I need it to do the Lord's work. Now where does she keep them bottles? I bring the bottle to my lips, but all is frozen within. Not a drop for poor Wilbert.

The droning continues, each voice buzzing over the other, and then I remember the bees deep in the hollow log beyond the birch grove. Eli leads me there. The golden light blinds me until I'm no longer sure if I'm watching the bees and dreaming I'm here or if I'm here in the snow dreaming I'm watching the bees. And it's then I hear the girls. Their light voices buzzing higher than all the rest.

Me, Me, Me . . . Do you smell that? Do you Jane? Momma's making potato pancakes! Get out of bed . . . I don't want to . . . Not even if she gives you extra syrup? . . . Okay, okay. What's that sound, Alice? . . . I don't know . . . It's the snow speaking to us. Can you

hear it? . . . It sounds like people calling. It's so soft I can barely hear it . . .
It's loud to me. Do you hear the drunk preacher? He says we're sinners . . . I
hear Momma calling. She says we better clean up . . . I don't want to clean.
I want to play. Come on, Alice, see if you can find me . . . Why is it dark if
we're awake? . . . You can't see? . . . Not very well . . . I think we're dreaming
. . . We've never dreamed together before . . . Yes, we have. Remember that
time we almost drowned in the river? . . . That's you that nearly drowned,
Jane . . . Yeah, but you dreamed it, too. Let's climb to the surface and make
snow angels! Let's make a city of tunnels! Look, there's Killian lying in the
snow beside the river! He can help us . . . Momma's going to get mad if
we don't get moving . . . No, she won't. She's always nicer when Daddy's
gone . . . My stomach's growling . . . I can't hear anything but the voices.
And the horses. Do you see the white horses, Alice? They're beautiful . . .
Come on, Jane. I'm hungry . . . You're always hungry. I'm going to ride the
white horses. Tell Momma I'll be along soon . . . She's not going to like it!

The longer I lay in the snow the more confused the voices get inside
my brain until the buzzing turns to stinging and I can no longer
hear myself anymore. My head is swollen so big. They fly inside
my head. Voices buzzing, flying, louder and louder. And it's then I
realize I'm a voice, too.

I tell myself I know the way home, but all I hear is the roiling
voices. And so I search. For days I wander looking for my body,
hoping to wake from the dream, but the more I search, the harder
I struggle, the more the dream ensnares me. I tell myself I know
the way, but then I don't know. The crooked mountain calls, and I
stumble beneath the killing cliff where the roan waits. Why don't I
recognize the smell of flesh decaying to madness?

I stagger forward, frost clinging to my eyes, blurring my vision.
The buzzing stretching before me with each step.

Dressed for hunting, my brother sits upon a rock. His rifle slung
upon his back. I see him clearly now, though I'm not sure if it's in
my mind's eye or my real ones.

I pull my hanky from out of my overalls and realize only then that I'm not wearing a coat. I hold the hanky before me. Blood drips from it, making great red spots that spread outward in the snow. A hawk cries overhead. I love hawks, especially the red-tailed ones. The way they spread their wings so wide in the sky, like nothing can hurt them.

"Why don't you just leave here," somebody yells. But I can't tell if it's my brother or another one of the voices. I suppose it no longer matters.

And then the buzzing stops. There is a rustling in the pines. The urine and burnt cedar smell of musk. The soft crunch of snow beneath dreamfooted hooves. The buck stands tall behind me. The one thing I know. Hot breath breaking the hoary air.

There's another sound. A loud one, and at first I think he's shot the buck, but I turn and it's still standing. Maybe it was the hawk. I search the heavens for a glimpse. The play of sunlight on red feathers dazzles.

The thick smell of pine struggles upward through snow, a gift. I smile as my tomb falls about me. Taking a handful of snow, pressing it to my feverish face, I slip through my deerskin boots.

The glade is clear and calm. Columbines blooming in the grassy patches. The beaver damn rises before me in its futile attempt to block the river. The mountain crooks silent. Eli stands above me, his smell strong—like a horse.

He is crying as he kneels in the snow by my side. I wonder if he sees me or if, like me, he is trapped in this dream.

"What happened?" I ask.

He takes my hand in his and lowers his head, praying beside me. "Why'd you have to come here?" he asks. Behind my question lies another question.

He stays with me for what seems like forever, and then he looks to the sky. But I don't think he sees the hawk because he gets up and runs away, west along the river.

The wet snow seeps through my britches. But it's not cold. Not cold at all, as my white tomb grows red. The hawk flies to me. He takes off his coat of feathers and lays it upon me. I gaze into his sharp, brown eyes, and I know he will not fly anymore. I feel sad, but there's nothing I can do. It's his choice, and he makes it freely.

I don't like the color of my grave. Too bright. Shiny. Not like the red of the hawk's wings. But that's okay, because I spread my wings, and the sky that falls on me is blue as I look down at the self that was me.

Circling above, like the hawk, I see my brother, Eli, running ever higher through the valley, and I want to laugh because the grave can't hold me. Will it hold you? I want to ask him. Will it hold you?

HANDS
Nell | *Colorado*

He asked me if I was happy, and I didn't know what to say.

He asked if I was proud of my work as a midwife. That I could answer.

"Then you are happy," he said.

He brought daisies to place inside the coffins. I didn't know where he could have found them. But somehow he did. He said he'd heard about the avalanche, about the deaths in the mining camp, and he'd come back to do what needed to be done.

I could swear his hand graced my forehead though he remained several feet away.

"I bring you a gift," he said. I thought the daisies were the gift.

Being old friends, Henry welcomed him into our home.

"The past is forgotten," Henry said.

"No," he replied.

Henry stared back at him, waiting for something less mysterious. "You always were a strange one, Wallace," he said.

The snow melted quickly, so that the tunnels were no longer safe to walk through. But it was not a matter of safety alone. After the avalanche, the people avoided the tunnels, and those few who traveled them said they heard voices whispering to them through the snow and ice. I had enough voices in my head, and so I stayed within my house.

Wallace suggested burying the entire camp in the center of town; he said the miners lived separately but they didn't have to die that way.

They stored the dead in Pete Myers' food locker, since most of the food was gone anyway. They said that they'd bury them where they lived up on the face of La Nana as soon as the snow melted and the ground thawed.

And the day after the last of the dead were found, carted to town, and stored in the food locker, the town went about its business, most of which consisted of sending the men to nearby towns for whatever food could be spared. Meanwhile, the women worked to prepare the church and the school for use once again.

I did not join them. My hold was slipping. Why work to bring life into the world when it is so easily lost? My life started with Alice and Jane, and now I felt it might end there.

Henry lost himself in the business of reorganizing the town. Giving orders, rebuilding structures that had collapsed under the weight of the snow. Yet soon these patchwork measures were not good enough for him. He wanted to make Seven Falls bigger and better. And so he called together the townsfolk to begin work on a library and, even, an art gallery. Henry said that nothing could slow down progress. I told him his progress was nothing but another form of snow.

For a week or more Wallace stayed with us, sleeping in the guest room while I slept upstairs, neither speaking a word, neither acknowledging the intimacy of air we shared, our mouths falling to confusion.

Then he stood at the foot of my bed, so tall I didn't know how he could fit in the room.

"I know only the odd things you grant me," he said, breaking the silence.

I don't know how long I lay there with him looking at me. I don't even know if it was day or night, though I assume it was day for Henry was gone. I could not look away.

"Come with me," he said. "Down the Blue, there's a valley. Come with me there."

"I cannot leave," I told him. "I'm bound by my breath to this place."

"Each time we breathe," he said. "We exhale the world."

"And what about the children?" I asked. "What about the others?"

"I've got lots of land," he said. "I'm giving it away to the first people who settle there."

"Henry," I said. One word, almost an afterthought.

"He can come if he likes. He is welcome."

"He will stay."

"Yes."

It was then he laid his hand upon my chest. My heart rushed, but not for want of him. His gesture was different.

"You are still a bird," he said.

It was then I decided why not love him. His hands were so large, so capable. It would be easy to fall into those hands.

THE STAGES OF COAL
HENRY | *Colorado*

Organic matter left in wet, acidic conditions does not rot completely but instead turns to soft, fibrous peat. Over eons, layer upon layer of sediments force out the moisture and squash the peat making smooth, brown coal. Yet still greater pressure turns that soft, brown rock into hard, black bituminous coal. But that is not enough. The final stage is anthracite, pressed so tightly together it nearly explodes in flame.

I have been buried for far too long.

Her visit struck my hard surface with the unwelcome news of what was essential. She asked me if I wanted to go with her. She told me we could all live together, that there was room for all of us. Time for all of us. She said she would be taking the children. Had I been porous, her words might have reached me.

Controlled blows can split a rock into a useful tool, fine-grained quartz into an implement for digging. What does it matter which way we face? What does it matter if we follow the rising blue?

What does it matter if we walk toward the sun or away from it to build our own? There is enough fire within my compressed body to heat the world. What does it matter if I'm split, if I shatter into a thousand pieces? Those pieces will still burn.

STORIES
KILLIAN | *Colorado*

Saturday is baking day, Sunday church, Monday wash, Tuesday clean the house, Wednesday canning, Thursday picking raspberries, Friday chickens.

The day before Catherine dies, Mother sees Jesus with his hands over her. The neighbor has to shake her back to her senses. Even then, Mother swears she saw what she saw. When Josephine dies, Mother cries for a month. She thinks nobody knows because the baby's inside her, but I know. She looks right at me one morning after she's done crying and asks, "Killian, how did you know?" But I don't have an answer.

Catherine says, "Mother, I'm going to die tomorrow," and then she does.

Chores: chop wood, clean chicken coop, spread manure, clean manure stalls. Hiding Places: chicken coop, hayloft, the dry spot under the porch, the well.

The cellar's full from one end to the other with mother's canned peaches.

Pebbles glittering in the rain. Every time I pick one up it stops glittering.

A cat stiff on the side of the road. Its eyes eaten out.

Sitting in the hayloft, eating green apples.

Catherine's coffin in the house. People praying over the body.

No matter how bad the winter, the flowers always return.

Muskrats on the bank, diving in just as you catch sight of them. I worry they'll eat my toes.

Lying under the elm or by the river, gazing up at the clouds and seeing the shapes. Sometimes you float away.

All the Christmas cookies are hidden in the guestroom. The entire room is full of cookies. You can smell them all through the house.

Mother says that the angels are always near, protecting us. We are never afraid.

When it snows, we make angels. Then we tunnel under the snow and spend all day there. Sometimes the angels get destroyed.

We drink out of a ladle that hangs on a nail by the sink. Uncle Frank takes the ladle because he forgets, and then we have to search all over the house for it.

Eli draws a line in the sand and lays the chickens so that their eyes are looking down that line, then he chops their heads off, and the chickens go running headless, blood spurting everywhere.

Father and Uncle Robert play music and everyone dances. Those are my favorite times with Father.

Mother calls the cinnamon rolls "snails." I try to imagine what snails taste like when I eat them, but it never works. The cinnamon fills my mouth.

Sleigh bells ringing outside on Christmas Eve.

Uncle Frank is Santa. I'm sure. He is.

Sometimes, when I wake, there are little gifts under my pillow, for no reason. One morning I'll find chalk, another morning a pinecone, a shell, a rock polished to a shine, a pebble with my initials painted on it. Even a stick carved to look like an Indian arrow. And sometimes nothing at all, which also seems special, after days of finding something. I'm pretty sure it's Uncle Frank that does this.

Every Saturday and Sunday, as soon as they wake, Webb and Molly check beneath their pillows. They are used to the game now. Sometimes I don't put anything there. This morning they each find a piece of string. They spend all morning playing in the spot between the bed and the wall.

Webb's string becomes a snake, then a king, and finally a great dragon raining fire on all he sees. Molly's string is a girl named Alky, who is later transformed into a princess. I get dizzy if I stay and watch.

Sometimes they turn to me, stepping out of their world to ask me if I want to play. I kneel down beside them, but no matter how hard I try I can't quite seem to enter the space they've created. Molly says that I'm still like a kid so I can do it. She says that if I can fly I can surely do this. And there are mornings when I feel the shining air about me and can almost see where I'm going. But so many times I can't. I guess I'm mostly adult after all.

You've got to believe in something, Uncle Frank says. That's what makes the world magic. And Catherine believes him. I believe him, too.

And I believe in Uncle Frank's stories. I know they are magic.

So I tell my stories every night to Molly and Webb, even Henry Jr. when he'll listen. I believe in the stories. I believe when I see Molly's eyes go wide as soon as I tell how I grab onto that giant snake, and it pulls me down its hole. I believe when I see Webb jump up with excitement when I tell how I walk the bottom of the river, talking with the fish, gathering stones for my house. Stories are the promise of life I give to the children. And they in turn give it back to me.

A THAWING AND A MELTING
Narrator/Killian | *Colorado*

Float again on the currents of Killian's imagination. Gaze with him as he spies the river from high above, sees it sharper than ever before. Watch the ripples appear and reappear through patches in the ice. Each time they are different. Just as this story would not be the same if you heard it again. It's as if the water is made up of many rivers, each breaking from the other, then joining, breaking and joining, swirling one about the other, rising up from the darkness along the bottom, then going down again, each swirl making its own pattern, yet all moving toward the same end.

Fly west as we follow his brother's tracks along the river between La Nana and her sister. Look closely as Eli digs a cave in the snow, a hole that will not last. Even now the ice drips from the roof. He backs himself in and curls up to wait. And we wonder if he can hear the voices following, angry voices with guns. They follow the tracks as we do. Eli is an expert woodsman and could cover the tracks if he wished. Even in the snow, there are ways. But he wants to be caught. He waits for them. Ready to fight from his hole. And he knows what any trapper knows: the cornered animal is the most dangerous because it has nothing to lose. He will shoot at them until they shoot back. And that, we think, is what he wants. Then the wind catches our wings, and we turn away.

Henry straddles a roof beam on the new town hall. We call down to him, but he does not hear. He is entirely focused on his work, hammering against the purple dusk. Stripped of his jacket and tie, we barely recognize him. He looks so different, so determined. Sweat pools under his arms even though it's near freezing. And then we spot the silk handkerchief wrapped around the handle of the hammer as he lays it down to wipe his brow, and we understand why he remains.

Look there, walking along the Blue. It's Wallace and Nell. And there, ducklings trailing behind: Henry Jr., Webb, and Molly. Oh, how we wish to scoop up Molly and follow. How we'd like to see Webb fly once more. They look happy, we're almost sure they do, for they are heading to their new home.

And where is our home? How will we find it? Already the voices swirl about us. *I think there's even a little syrup left.* We fight the voices, wanting our freedom. *Let me dust the snow off you, let me warm you in my hands.* But then we know it's useless. *I know Lucy will give me a drink.* The voices have always been part of us. *Do you hear the drunk preacher?* And we part of them. *I don't know. It seems the more I clean the dirtier things get.* So, like the sky, we listen. *As soon as I find my tobacco, I'm getting the hell out of here.* We feel the rhythm of the air about us. *She knows I need it to do the Lord's work.* We soar higher, and the sun slips through us. *Do you see the white horses, Alice? They're beautiful.* And we know it is always now. It has always been now.

The greatest mysteries have the simplest answers. The snow melts, and we melt with it. The ice thaws, and we join. *There's never been a whale as big as this one.* The present is falling backward, voices crashing one into the other, and we cannot hold. *Frank, you son-of-a-bitch, you were never a sailor!* Time does not exist unless we will it, and it is only our habit that makes it so. *Are you sleeping, Killian, like the deer?* No, Catherine, sleep is different. *Different how?* We don't know. *It all started the day your Uncle Robert gave me permission to visit his sister* . . . The harsh tang of sweat, hops, and woodsmoke . . . Thick tendrils of web hang about us, drifting back and forth in the light air above the rafters . . . He puts the pipe in his mouth and puffs, considering . . . Through the smoke, we can barely make out the shadowy figures on the bench below. Who is that man puffing on the pipe? . . . And the very next day your father was over at her house, sitting high atop his horse and talking with her through the window. I saw the

whole thing and couldn't believe it . . . Jake is that you? Who are
the children sitting beside you? We can scarcely remember . . . Was
that horse one of the crazy ones? . . . If we can't remember, how are
we supposed to finish the tale? How do we get the story right? . . .
Your Uncle Robert had just got himself a young team after making
a deal to buy this tavern. He was so proud he took Meg, I mean
your mother, for a ride down Main Street on a Sunday afternoon
. . . The tendrils float on the unseen currents, sometimes touching,
forming new versions of webs . . .

Look, now. Here's one more:

Meg emerges from behind the bar, three mugs of beer in each hand,
making her way through the crowd, laughing as one by one the
beers disappear, the last one going to a dark-haired man with gray
eyes. He smiles at her, gestures to the dance floor where a lone man
plays the accordion. She does a little jig for a moment, but then
waves him away, as if she thinks he must be joking. Her attention
turns toward another man sitting on the side bench beneath the
corn sheller. She makes her way to him, asking if she can share
the last bit of pie on his plate. He tamps his pipe and tucks it in
his pocket. He assures her that their children are all asleep. The
last remnant of the fudge scent wafts through the rafters. Then he
scoops up a forkful of the pie and places it in her mouth, delicately
wiping away the trace of raspberry that graces her lip.

It is then we understand. It doesn't matter if our memories are
real or if they are imagined. Our best hope is to dream, even if
imperfectly, who and what we are. To dream and tell the tale.

This is the part I don't like, Henry says, covering his ears.

Where does the story end?

In Nahoonkara.

Where does it begin?

Nahoonkara

About the Author

Peter Grandbois is the author of *The Gravedigger* (Chronicle Books, 2006), a Barnes and Noble "Discover Great New Writers" and Borders "Original Voices" selection as well as the hybrid memoir, *The Arsenic Lobster* (Spuyten Duyvil 2009). His essays and short fiction have appeared in magazines such as: *Boulevard, Narrative, Post Road, Gargoyle, Zone 3, Eleven Eleven, The Denver Quarterly, Word Riot, Pindeldyboz, and The Writer's Chronicle,* among others, and have been short listed for the Pushcart Prize. He serves as associate editor for *Narrative* magazine and is a professor of creative writing and contemporary literature at California State University in Sacramento.

Acknowledgments

Writing is, in the end, a solitary endeavor, but that endeavor and this book have been infinitely enriched by the generosity of the following people: Daniel Grandbois, Laird Hunt, Gary Isaacs, Brian Kiteley, Betsy Johnson-Miller, Doug Rice, Irene Vilar, Tanya Wilson, Amy Wright, and all my colleagues at the University of Denver who commented on the chapters in workshop. Thank you also to Mary Ellen Gilliland whose book on Frisco, Colorado, was invaluable to the writing of this book and to the members of the rock band 16hp whose haunting music provided inspiration throughout the creative process. Special thanks also go to Phil Brady and the staff at Etruscan Press for the strength of their vision and the warmth of their spirit.

Books from Etruscan Press

Founded in 2001 with a generous grant from the Oristaglio Foundation, Etruscan Press is a nonprofit cooperative of poets and writers working to produce and promote books that nurture the dialogue among genres, achieve a distinctive voice, and reshape the literary and cultural histories of which we are a part.

ETRUSCAN IS PROUD OF SUPPORT RECEIVED FROM

Bates-Manzano Fund

Council of Literary Magazines and Presses

The National Endowment for the Arts

New Mexico Community Foundation

Nin & James Andrews Foundation

The Ohio Arts Council

Ruth H. Beecher Foundation

The Stephen & Jeryl Oristaglio Foundation

The Wean Foundation

Wilkes University

Youngstown State University

etruscan press
www.etruscanpress.org

Etruscan Press books may be ordered from

Consortium Book Sales and Distribution
800-283-3572
www.cbsd.com

Small Press Distribution
800-869-7553
www.spdbooks.com

Etruscan Press is a 501(c)(3) nonprofit organization.
Contributions to Etruscan Press are tax deductible
as allowed under applicable law.
For more information, a prospectus,
or to order one of our titles,
contact us at books@etruscanpress.org